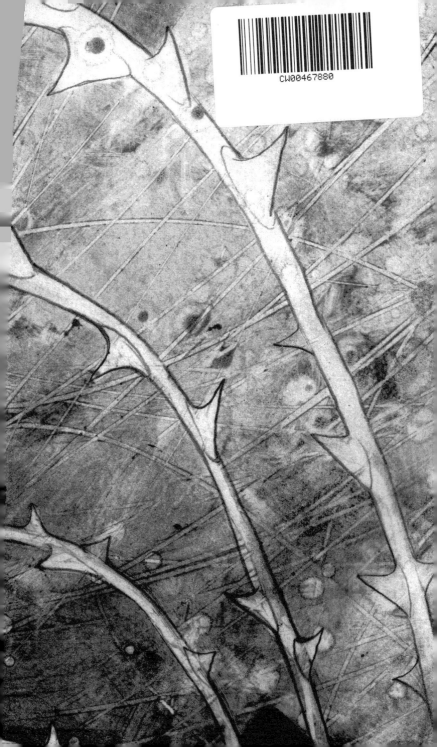

The Bank of Dreams & Nightmares
20 Rax Lane, Bridport, DT6 3JJ

www.thebankofdreamsandnightmares.org

Published September 2022 by
The Bank of Dreams & Nightmares

Creative learning manager / Editor
Janis Lane

Volunteer story mentors
Nick Goldsmith
Raja Jarrah
Eleanor James
Amberley Carter

Partner teacher
Liz Launder

Designer
Spike Golding

Illustration
Staffan Gnosspelius

ISBN 978-1-7397340-1-5
Printed in Exeter by Imprint books
Distributed by The Bank of Dreams & Nightmares

SPIRALLING

A SLOW DESCENT INTO MADNESS

Stories by writers from
Sir John Colfox School in Dorset

FOREWORD

STOP READING THIS BOOK!

It isn't safe. Place it carefully back where you found it, and walk away. You can still survive.

No?

Fine. Don't say I didn't warn you. Not that the "friendly" person from The Bank of Dreams & Nightmares adequately warned me. 'Would you like to read some fiction by year nine pupils of Sir John Colfox school?' they asked.

Year nine, I thought. Children, I thought. A bit of light reading, I thought. What could possibly go wrong?

The death toll is high, the crimes unspeakably brutal. This collection of short stories, flash fiction and kennings poetry is anything but light. Over the coming pages, you will meet demons straight from the bowels of hell, artificial intelligence, ghosts, spirits, murderers, mythological beings and even Death itself. You will be transported to the future, the past, and stuck in time-loops. You'll witness forbidden family secrets, jealousy, betrayal and revenge. You will – perhaps most terrifyingly of all – get lost in Ikea.

For all its delicious darkness, there's tenderness and hope. Tropes are subverted, and characters are made real. It's endlessly surprising. The careful editorial attention that has gone into these creative works is clear to see, and these young writers were not alone in their efforts. The Bank of Dreams & Nightmares is a charity whose sole mandate is to offer creative writing enrichment to under-resourced children, helping to elevate their writing and to give it purpose and an audience. The possibilities are endless and, in this case, have led to the (macabre, unsettling, eerie…) anthology you hold in your hands. I've warned you not to read it. But if you dare, I hope you enjoy it as much as I did.

Nathan Filer
May 2022

KENNING POEMS

A Kenning is a two-word phrase that describes something, rather than actually naming it. It is essentially a riddle and creates a special kind of metaphor, commonly used in Anglo-Saxon poetry. One of the most famous is the epic Old English poem, Beowulf, written in the tradition of Germanic heroic legend and saga. The author wanted to convey powerful imagery; in Beowulf the sea is known as the whale-road and battle-sweat refers to blood.

We tasked our Colfox cohort to produce Kenning Poems, keeping in mind the eerie theme. Their mastery of metaphors was impressive, evoking a real sense of unease and the unknown with phrases such as sight-givers and body-formers.

Enjoy decoding their eerie 'riddles'.

BY TOBY

Light -flashes below the brick-surrounders

Feet-upholders shift beneath me, making a dreadful scream

Melting-flames flicker, then grey-wanderer escapes

Then shivers my body-formers feel ice-stuck

BY LAURA, MANI & SUMMER

The night sky-lantern

Reflecting its face on the

Moving-mirror. The silence

Blanketing on the beach. The

Fear-harbourer lurking in

The shadows. The wind-whistler

Tugging on her hair

SAKURA BLOOM
BY TOBY WILLIAMS

Prologue

I sprinted. Screams bellowed behind me getting quieter and quieter. Could this be less people crying or me getting further away? Tears streaming from my eyes, my mind scared after seeing my mother and father being killed before my eyes. I should have stayed at home like they said. I shouldn't have made them vulnerable. It's all my fault but I'll do what they last said.
"RUN, RUN," they had chimed, "Get out of here."

Blood stained my hair; I used a purple clip to fasten it behind my head. I wore a delicate wandering Samurai kimono with purple Sakura pattern. Her sword had flown into the air when she died. That monster needed to be killed.

Sow

I looked at the Katana, my mother's blade. She had crafted it herself with such an intricate design. Our family had the power to block a sense of an enemy. It was useful for slipping out of situations. I saw my reflection, the colour in my eye so intricate and lilac like the blade.

I stopped admiring the blade, stood up, and walked down the hollow-way. Many people had walked down here. The stone beneath me had been worn away. I got to the end of the hollow-way to the dead-gathering. My clothes brushed past the headstones, and I stepped towards the massive Sakura tree that was in the middle. I picked a flower from the tree and went over to my mother's grave. I placed the bright petals on the ridge of the headstone. My father was buried with my mother, but he died when I was young. I took my gaze off the grave and looked towards the other ones. So many dead and no-one coming to see them.

Something caught my gaze. Something pure white, small, but was out of my sight to take a good look. The last people stopped coming here a few years ago. I wasn't alone.

Seed

A figure emerged from one of the gravestones. I did not recognise them – they were probably from the town. They were small, had a beard, and were dressed in vine and plant patterned clothes. They walked over to me and said, "Still grieving, child?"

I was stunned by their question. *Have they been watching me all this time, and who are they?* Also, what was my answer? I just stay here. I still may be sad, but it's been a few years.

"Do you want to stay here or defeat the Iracundus that caused your town so much harm?" said the strange being.

I gasped inside. *Was he talking about the monster?*

I looked down at my Katana I had scabbarded, and the handguard shaped like a perfect Sakura flower.

"Destroy," I said quietly to myself.

I accepted his offer, but little did I know how much I needed to do.

Leaf

It was a month since I started training with Mr Chidendro and I had learnt a lot too: that there were special techniques that people learn to kill Iracundus. They were based on elements, and nature was the first one; the others were just branch-offs to suit their style. I happened to have the only nature elemental teaching me. The different stuff I can do as a nature user; I can grow poisonous plants, healing vines to capture enemies.

The training was very hard on my body. I had to be physically and mentally strong. I also met lots of different element users so there was an electro, glacier, insect, vibration, and many more users.

Sprout

I began eating some miso soup, matcha mochi I had just made, when there was a report of an Iracundus causing mayhem. Iracundus had distinctive horns that if you break, you can strip them of power then kill them. I became used to the call-outs – I rarely had any trouble. I got myself ready, packed some food just in case of a long journey, and my Katana. I was ready to go, following the messenger bird to a town that looked like my old town, and a barrier just the same, but I knew how to pass through it. On the cobbled streets children cowered in houses but were intrigued to see someone outlandishly dressed coming in.

I heard a scream, then quiet. I knew they were close. I ran towards the sound to find the Iracundus. I was startled to find the same Iracundus, the monster in my old town. They dropped the terrified human and ran towards me.

"Oh, it's you, scared child, the one that didn't flinch and ran from the battlefield," said the Iracundus.

They had remembered me.

Stalk

Mount Kanna. It would be hard to think that a village would be there. However, being so isolated had its downsides; it was the perfect prey for evil. A crow's call was fading away, but my focus could not be stripped from me. The Iracundus had not changed. Same form, same attire. Come to think of it, they were much different to any other Iracundus I had seen. Most had more Kaiju forms but this one didn't. Were they the leader? Mist swirled around us.

"Have you come here for revenge?" they asked. "You wouldn't be the first."

They pointed to a body, which had been flung from a very large distance. Blood dripping from their mouth to rest on their lap. Barely twitching. I stammered. I was shaken by the gore in front of me. My breathing unnormalised, I almost went faint. I shook myself into concentration.

"They were rather weak though," the Iracundus said, walking over to the body.

They caressed its face like a kind of weird psychopathic killer.

Then, in just a flash of movement their body was thrown up, falling apart from what it was connected to, blood splattering around them. I was still stuck in place, as if the mist around me were shackles. I took a deep breath and withdrew my sword.

"So, you are going to fight me, so it's not cowardice, which you have previously shown," they exclaimed.

I looked around me. Few plants were in sight but a forest not too far away. If I could distract them enough to get them there I might stand a chance. I launched my first attack, blade drawn to side slice, but they dodged, leaping into the air. They summoned two sickles in their hands; they were red and writhing as if they were on fire. They launched towards me, and the next five minutes would be the hardest time trying to stay alive. You could hear the clashing and slashes of my Katana. My body was nearly worn out and they left no gap for me to rest or recover.

Finally, we got to the forest and I reached and enlarged a pair of vines. I then wrapped it around them just revealing their head. They struggled but couldn't move. I prepared myself to strike their horns, but in a blaze of flames they ignited themselves and half the forest was ablaze. I couldn't do anything; They had burned the vine which had engulfed them. Gone. And that was my big plan now turned to ash. Then the mist swirled away, and a voice spoke.

"Giving up already?"

Bulb

I recognised that voice, it was...

"Hey! Looks like we made it just in time," said another recognisable voice, "Do you have any faith in who your mentor is?"

They walked in front of me in a uniform that matched their weapons. There were six of them. All I had met, each representing a different technique: glacier, boulder, electro, gale, vibration, aqua, and spirit.

"At least let us get fully on the battlefield before you attack," said the aqua user.

The Iracundus took no time in waiting for introductions, instead sprang into action with their sickles blazing. They were immediately drenched in water by the aqua user. The Iracundus was shocked but said, "You really think your feeble water can douse my flames?"

They set themselves alight to evaporate the water. However, there was still residue left on their body.

"See, look at me, I'm invinci...," said the Iracundus, but being injected by the glacier user.

"Watch your tone."

With a flick of his sword, the water residue turned into strange ice and expanded. The Iracundus was shocked again but in a weird way like they didn't know the world around them. It was the vibration user bombarding them, which made their insides bubble and fizz. There was also something holding onto the Iracundus and pulling them apart. The spirit user was configuring their ghosts and poltergeists to do what was happening. I was shocked but amazed how brilliantly well they were working together. But I hadn't really done anything. The gale user spoke to me.

"We will go for the horns, then you go after and take their neck."

I was a little shocked at their voice at first.

"So, don't let us down," said the electro user.

"Are you ready?" said the gale user, determinedly.

I smiled and replied, "Yes!"

They launched into action, the air reacting seconds later. The Iracundus was beginning to heat up, then they sliced the horns off. Now, it was my turn. I prepared my Katana in hand, the Iracundus still dazed. I ran as fast as I could. I began to make my blade tear through their neck, but it got stuck. I needed to push harder. Then the others went to their weapons and helped the neck detach. It bounced on the floor, rolling. Then it disintegrated itself and the dust was carried along the wind. They were finally defeated.

ECHOES OF SILENCE
BY MANi CHALMERS

They sat together. The candles burnt slowly; she watched as the wax fell to the ground. His eyes burnt into her back. Amaru could picture the look on his face. A patronising smirk accompanied by a pair of cold eyes.

* * *

She woke up. The sharp stab of the rock she had been sleeping on made itself clear. She was not with him; she was still alone. The chatter of the forest grew in volume as she washed her sleep away. The dew of the morning sat contentedly on the grass, occasionally dripping to the ground. Her lack of sleep only increased the unnecessary noise. The sky was still dark with no promise of the sun making an appearance. Good. She considered waiting for him there – the towering trees offered her an ounce of comfort. She abandoned that idea as a nest of birds began to chirp.

"Hah, can you imagine?" she chuckled to herself. She wouldn't let him find her in a place where life and noise lived peacefully together. No. He would think she was changing. Changing for him, and that idea made her stomach churn.

She stood up. Her mind was already awake and was patiently waiting for her body to catch up. The clouds grew dark and the rain was rearing its ugly head. Her shoes had given up a while ago and the cold grass irritated her toes. Once again he appeared in her thoughts. And then the rain came.

"Of course," she said to herself.

Amaru tilted her face towards the sky, and she let the rain wash it clean. And for the first time in a long time, she smiled. But it was short lived. Suddenly her foot fell into a hole and a surge of pain rushed through her. And she did the most human thing she had done for a while: she screamed. The wail echoed throughout the forest, washing out any other noises that were present. The pain she felt soon turned into frustration and her scream dripped with anger. It was over. He would come and she would have to go back. She fell to her knees and held herself in a loving embrace. She let the tears fall freely. She was not ashamed of herself – it was only a matter of time before something she did drew him near.

Her eyes began to close, and the sweet relief of sleep gave her some solace. It would distract her from the throbbing pain she felt in her foot.

* * *

The sun was beginning to set when she awoke. Her foot no longer ached and that's how she knew he was there. She hoped to fall back to sleep but her eyes yearned to see him again. He watched as her eyes fell on his and he could not stop the smile that now played on his lips.

"I have missed you."

The words came out rather stiffly.

"No, you haven't," she said, her eyes still trained on his. Confusion came over him and that quickly turned to anger.

"Why, why won't you let me love you?"

His voice quivered with rage.

"Because you can't, and I won't let you convince yourself you can. You don't control me. I owe you nothing." Amaru's voice rang out and her breath quickened.

A blank expression appeared on his face. And then it was dark, and the deafening quiet had returned to her.

He didn't know how long it had been since he had got her back. Although there was a comfort in her presence, he ached for more. And despite his want for her in this life he knew what he needed to do to ensure their lives stayed entwined.

The gentle glow of the candles illuminated the cold room around her.

"Are you ready?" he asked.

The blankness of his expression put her on edge.

"I'm not sure..."

Her voice trailed off. Amaru's eyes fell onto the door that lay behind him. The darkness of it entranced her. The quiet it gifted was beautiful. And suddenly, all the irritation this life presented fell away.

He reached for her hand, and she took it willingly. The door was in view. He hesitated, but she never stopped. They walked through, never once turning back.

THE KHAN MAKR*
BY COE TIGG

A young boy around the age of 15 opened his weary eyes to reveal a rundown, abandoned hospital. He stood up, revealing his 5'5 stature. He looked down at his rather muscly arm to see a large tube running into it. He ripped it out with much ferocity. A strange blue substance rushed out of his wrist. He took a good look around the room, assessing the situation.

Large cracks in the wall represented a state of decay. Blue tiles laid across the wall, only barely holding on. A large metal dish displayed above him, which one could only assume used to be a light.

As he started to walk around the room he flinched from the broken shards of glass on the floor. He heard a flickering behind him, and he turned around; a hologram of a woman appeared.

She had the words UAC written on her uniform. She announced in a joyful upbeat tone:

"The cleansing of earth is a necessary process on the path to a better future."

Flynn stood there for a few seconds, trying to make sense of what just happened. The lady appeared again.

"Our friends won't walk on tainted ground. Earth must be purified first."

Our friends? Who's our friends? Another sound appeared behind him. This time not a flickering, but a groaning. He turned around and a pale figure stood before him. One of his arms was missing and it stumbled and fell as it edged closer. Its flaky skin fell behind it and it had a uniform similar to the lady's, with the same letters UAC written on it.

Suddenly the beast lunged towards him and clenched its teeth into Flynn's arm as Flynn struggled for his life. A bark was heard in the distance and a pit-bull tackled the creature to the floor. Flynn took the opportunity to finish it off and grabbed one of the scalpels on the doctor's tray, plunging it into the creature's head.

"Jack," Flynn cried, "I'm so glad you're alive!"

The dog jumped around in excitement, licking Flynn's face. After a few minutes of reuniting, Flynn and Jack decided it was time to continue onwards. They walked out of the room they were originally in and stumbled across an office.

As he entered, the computer replayed the footage of a robotic figure.

"My name is Samuel L. Hayden. I am the founder of the UAC and creator of Argent energy. With the energy shortage there was on earth I devoted my life to create a sustainable energy source. We set out a location – Mars – in hope we'd recover something. Then we found it, Argent energy, pure essence of hell. Using this, we saved the planet, but we also destroyed it. I was arrogant to tamper with things beyond my understanding. A portal opened from hell releasing the downfall of humanity. If you're still alive, take this AI V.E.G.A. and listen closely. To close the portal is a must."

The computer shut off and a new figure appeared. She was tall and floaty. She was white with a yellow ring around her head. She too was almost robotic looking. She looked almost angelic but with a demonic resonance about her.

"I am the Khan Makr also known as the Icon of Sin. I am God of hell and leader of the punishment of earth. Samuel Hayden: he's falling, and there is no longer anything stopping our purge. The UAC is over, Makr rule, and their souls have been taken to Netrovod to be harvested. 87% of earth has been laid to waste with the numbers rapidly increasing. This is not the last announcement."

The Khan Makr disappeared. Flynn and Jack stood in awe and confusion. Flynn looked over at a small chip on the left labelled V.E.G.A. He picked it up and examined it. The chip then disappeared out of Flynn's hand. It took a bit for him to process what happened. Screams of fear and pain echoed through the corridors. His arms flailed about as his veins popped out of his arm. Flynn's entire body seized up and he froze. Finally, the pain stopped.

Flynn fell to the floor in a pool of sweat, coughing violently. Jack pressed into the corner in shock.

"Hello, I'm V.E.G.A.," a monstrous voice bounced around Flynn's head.

"Get. Out. Of. My. Head." Flynn gritted his teeth through the pain.

"Sensing high levels of stress. Enacting protocol 73."

V.E.G.A. continued to echo through Flynn's skull.

Flynn felt himself get sleepy as he stumbled and fumbled around the room, until he finally collapsed on the floor, motionless.

Jack finally unfroze and dash towards him licking his face and nudging his shoulder Flynn drifted further away until it all went dark.

Flynn woke up with a jolt. After noticing Flynn arise, Jack leapt around in joy. Flynn responded with a large hug and a belly rub.

"Vitals stable," V.E.G.A. said.

Instead of freaking out, this time Finn took a deep breath and spoke.

"Who are you, V.E.G.A.?"

"I am an artificial intelligence known as V.E.G.A., created and designed by Samuel L. Hayden."

"Okay I don't think I can get rid of you so I might as well accept you."

Flynn stood up and brushed off his clothes.

"What I don't understand is what I'm supposed to be doing now."

"You are Flynn Madook of Earth. Age 15, blood type 0. You have been put under several experiments by the Khan Makr, giving you unknown abilities and enhanced bodily functions. Earth is corrupted by hell and it's up to you to save it."

V.E.G.A. finished his analysis, leaving Flynn even more confused.

V.E.G.A. spoke up once again.

"Your first sign of action would be to exit this facility."

Flynn walked out of the office. *Finally, something that makes sense*, he thought.

"Downloading area layout to neuro patterns."

As V.E.G.A. said this Flynn felt a sudden rush through his body as images flashed through his head. He suddenly knew every single detail about the facility he was in.

"Whoa, what was that?"

Flynn stood in awe.

"I have hooked my mainframe into your thermal system making my memory yours - however I am not at full function. One more chip is required for my full ability - marking its location now."

A bright yellow marker appeared on his mind. It was a room not too far from there: only a couple of rooms down. Flynn beckoned over Jack to follow him. Jack bounded along happily. Flynn continued down the corridor until they were met with a looming figure at the end of it. It was the same creature from before, only this time in uniform and with a crest on its head.

"V.E.G.A., what is that?" Flynn said desperately.

24

"That is a cultist, praiser of the Khan Makr; they are fragile enemies with low attack."

Flynn looked down at his arm expecting to see a bite but was shocked to find a completely healthy arm. Before Flynn could question it V.E.G.A. spoke up.

"Wherever they go, cultists spread demonic energy causing it to become corrupt and demonic. This can be defeated through..."

Before V.E.G.A. could finish, the creature crept towards Flynn. With almost no hesitation Flynn outstretched an arm and the creature's head was splattered across the wall. Flynn looked down at his arm in disbelief; blood trickled down it. He felt more alive, as if before he was merely warming up. This must be the power V.E.G.A. was talking about, he thought. Jack seemed ecstatic at the fact of this happening, yelping, and barking in joy. Flynn laughed.

"Calm down before someone hears us."

Flynn continued down the hall until he was outside the room V.E.G.A. marked. Just before Flynn touched the handle an even larger creature rounded the corner. This one was different to the first one. It was exceedingly larger with bulking muscles and a red flare in its eyes. It was much faster as well.

Before Flynn even registered its existence he was sent flying to the end of the corridor. Pain ruptured through his body, and he coughed up blood all over the floor. Jack was barking hysterically at the beast. It didn't even acknowledge his existence and walked towards Flynn. Flynn tried to get up but collapsed again helplessly. Its silver skin shimmered as a large and fiery blade extended out of its head. Its head had two large protruding horns. It didn't have a nose, just two holes which would shoot snot at them with every breath. It raised its arm ready to strike. Jack leapt up and sunk his teeth into the demon. It didn't ignore him this time and lifted its foot to squash Jack. He instinctively dodged out of the way and attacked again. Jack wasn't so lucky this time and was stopped mid-air, a large hellish blade streaking into his stomach and out of his mouth. The demon lifted its blade, cutting Jack clean in two.

Flynn couldn't believe it. He wouldn't believe it. Jack, the only friend he'd had for his entire life now just a deformed pile of sleugh on the floor. Flynn yelled in anger, all recent pain gone. He leapt up towards the creature and knocked it in the stomach followed quickly by a knee to the jaw. He ripped the left horn clean off the beast and smashed it against its head. The demon was dazed and confused, unable to comprehend what just happened. Flynn continued to punish the beast by pushing it to the floor, pinning it down, and stamping its elbow backwards, causing the bone to shatter and arm to fall off. Flynn used the beast's blade to stab it right in the chest and lifted it, cutting the creature in two, just like Jack.

Flynn stood panting. He was now powered by pure rage. All. Of. Them. Must. Die. He stormed into the second room and grabbed V.E.G.A.'s final download. Compared to last time, Flynn had no reaction to the chip entering his body, and just carried on through the building.

"The Khan Makr is at the top of this building. She is attempting to use Argent energy to open other portals back to her home world."

Flynn walked back to the creature's remains and used V.E.G.A. to scan them.

"This is a being of hell, an extremely powerful demon fetched by the Khan Makr to assimilate you."

Flynn grunted and kicked its head across the floor. He looked up at the ceiling, then at Jack's remains.

"I'll make them pay; don't you worry."

He leapt up to the ceiling and bashed a hole clean through it. Flynn powered his way through the building, killing anything and everything in his path. He showed no mercy through his purge. He showed no sign of slowing down and only had one thing on his mind: destruction.

V.E.G.A. spoke once again.

"Your Crucible is nearby, an ancient weapon used by the Sentinels. It will be required to kill the Khan Makr."

Flynn turned to the markings on his map and sprinted towards it. He ploughed through walls and demons, leaving a path of destruction in his wake. He slowed to a stop as he reached a white, empty room, with a large glass container in the centre of it. Inside was a large red sword with large red energy discharges shooting from the blade. It was ancient, roughly embedded into the hilt. Flynn had no hesitation whatsoever and walked towards the weapon. V.E.G.A. spoke.

"You must carefully extract the Crucible so as not to destabilise it."

Flynn plunged his hand into the chamber, grasping hold of the Crucible and yanking it out. Large bursts of energy erupted from the tip, and Flynn felt the power flow through him. He felt almost God-like, as if he could take on the world. The sword shrunk down to fit the palm of his hand; the sword was long and parted into an arrow at the end of it.

"The Khan Makr is directly above us. If you wish to stop her now is your opportunity," V.E.G.A. said.

Flynn looked up once again and broke through the ceiling onto the roof. The Khan Makr stood before Flynn.

"Do you really think you can stop me? I created you. I can just as easily do the opposite."

Flynn grasped hard to the hilt of his sword. His burning rage only grew as the images of Jack flashed across his mind. He let out a cry of rage and leapt for the Khan Makr. He expected to pierce her heart, but instead passed right through her. A hologram? He felt a gush of wind behind him and looked down to a spear through his stomach. He turned around and saw the Khan Makr on the other side of the spear.

"Pitiful human," she muttered, and twisted the spear into him further.

Flynn turned to her. Pure rage was in his eyes as he snapped the spear in two. He lifted his sword to strike and brought it down swiftly onto the Khan Makr's head. She let out a screech like a banshee as the blade sank into her. She collapsed to the ground. Her lifeless body lay helplessly on the floor. Flynn smiled for a second before he remembered his wound. He vomited everywhere and fell to the floor in agony. All the rage keeping him alive previously had gone, leaving him once again just a normal boy.

THE PIANO AND THE FIGURE
BY SAMUEL BARTLETT

The man was trapped in the abandoned building. There was no way out. The man was trapped in the building because he saw a strange man walk in through the door, so he decided to see where he was going. But when he went in, the door slowly closed behind him, and then it jammed. That was the only way in. He walked all around the building but couldn't see anything. The windows were boarded up and the building was huge. It had been abandoned for years and was also very unsafe.

He didn't find the man either, even though he saw him go in there. It was an old stage where shows used to be performed. There was a grand piano in the main hall. It was very strange because that was all that was in there and it was in really good condition. But there were a lot of strange noises – sometimes they sounded like they were really close behind him but when he turned around he never saw anything. All he saw was the usual flaky paint, and decay everywhere.

He carried on, deeper into the abandoned theatre, and was getting closer to the stage. He was intrigued to know what was going to happen now. As soon as he walked up onto the stage it felt like he was being watched all around and he started to feel something very warm on the back of his neck. He suddenly turned around but there was nothing there. He also heard some very faint footsteps walk around him, and some laughing and cheering. He jumped off the stage and then everything suddenly fell silent. He walked up along the aisle and studied the piano. It looked brand new even though everything else around him was abandoned. He pressed a key and it worked straight away. The echo suddenly filled the whole entire building, and a sudden rush of fresh air flew through the building and then stopped. It felt like everyone in the world was watching him now.

He decided to explore upstairs and see what was happening there. There was an aisle straight down the middle and there were lots of rooms either side. He was walking through the corridor when he started to hear the piano downstairs playing a tune. He paused for a minute and hurried downstairs to see what was going on. He slowly crept into the main hall and realised there was no one playing the piano. The piano was playing itself. He walked over to it, and he touched one of the keys that was pushed down. The piano suddenly stopped playing There was quite a loud echo in the building now. Whatever was playing the piano was obviously very talented.

Suddenly there was a creak on the floorboards next to him – it sounded like a footstep. It sounded like someone was walking away from the piano. It was heading towards the stage. The man followed the footsteps. It had walked up onto the stage and into what looked like a prep room behind the stage. He walked in there, but it was a dead end and it was completely silent. He decided to carry on searching upstairs.

He walked upstairs and carried on walking through the aisle. He walked almost up to the end of the rooms, and it was then he saw the figure…

He said to the figure, "Hello."

The figure didn't say anything. He just sat there for some reason. Then the man said, "Who are you?"

There was a 10 second pause.

"I am Peter, one of the main characters; if you want to watch a performance, buy a ticket!"

He was very nervous now but wanted to find out more. It sounded like Peter thought there was still a show.

"Have you noticed the state of the building? This place closed down years ago!"

"How dare you; this building is perfectly safe and is ready to perform. If you don't like it, you can go!"

After talking for about quarter of an hour, he started to walk off but quickly turned back and took a photo of the figure. He didn't even realise! He walked back downstairs and said to himself, *Right, I must get out of here!* He picked up an iron bar and beat the wooden door down, dropped the bar, and ran off. He was very relieved once he managed to get out. He felt a sudden breath of fresh air go through his body. It felt like he hadn't been outside for years. He decided to never go back in again just in case he couldn't get out next time. He walked over to his Land Rover, got in, and drove off, leaving all the ghosts and figures behind.

THE DEVOURER
BY ELLA READ

Diary Entry
2022

....

There it was, the Beelitz Hospital. After years of tirelessly
searching, I was finally there. I couldn't contain my excitement, so
I almost flew over the barbed wire, pushing my way through bits
of damp wood and shuffled my way on the floor caked with glass;
the smell of disinfectant punched my nose, hitting me like a sucker
punch. I thought the dilapidated building was collapsing in on
itself. I pulled my torch from my coffin bag and began to study the

layout of this place, doors that laced the hallways. I opened doors I shouldn't have and I couldn't seem to close them.

Hallways piled on top of each other, forming a maze of despair and agony in one beautiful, horrific choir, and finally I found it. The room. By this time, I thought I was losing my mind. Hours passed, if not days, and finally it was here but what I didn't know was that when I opened that door it was like opening Pandora's box...

A cold feeling brushed through my body like thousands of needles piercing my skin, then nothing.

The room was desiccated, collapsed, forgotten by time: bluebottles raining down on me like snow, cobwebs dusting the room like a layer of glass; it was silent...too silent. I continued studying the room like hieroglyphics. A great sense of accomplishment turned to fear; I heard my name being whispered as it tried to taunt me...

"It's your fault she's dead."

Tears streamed down my face...

"You've found us, what will you do now?"

My fear turned into sadness and then into uncontrollable, absolute rage, consuming me from the inside out, then this horrendous force thrusted me back through a wall or two – I can't really remember – then nothing.

Barely able to catch my breath I scrambled to my feet, pushing the bricks and wood off my body. I grasped the cold, firm, wall, hobbling through the rubble.

"Persistent aren't you?"

The voice was different than before. It was deeper, more sinister.

I was knocked off my feet again, this time an agonising burning sensation wrapped around my ankles like scolding hot irons. I felt as if I was being pulled backwards. I grasped the floor, then the wood planks, my hands restlessly searching for something to grab onto. The pain was unbearable. My grip loosened…

My name was Kai McCall. I was 16 in 2022. It's now 2040 and I'm still 16, waiting for salvation.

GUILT
BY WiLL FiNK

I wake up in a subway station and I immediately feel a strong pain in my left leg. It sears through my body causing pain everywhere.

I'm a tall man. I was born in Helsinki in Finland. The last thing I remember was that my father died – he was only 63 – and then I was at his funeral and now I have woken up here. I have to get my leg out of this chair – it is stuck with something, but I don't know what. Now I see I am in the London underground, but something is missing. I realise it is empty and there is no stress. Something is wrong. This is Piccadilly Circus. It is packed every day.

The pain I feel when thinking about my father is practically unbearable. I grew up with him. He had always been there for me and now I feel as if I let him down. I'm not sure how – I can't quite remember – but I know I did in some way. Just thinking about him makes me hurt much more than my leg.

For the last 30 minutes I have been trying to slowly get my leg out from under this bin, but every movement is pain. When I move my leg it sends pain searing through my body, but I know I must move it to get out of this situation. In a minute I will just pull my leg out of this bin.

"Three, two, one… Aarghh"

I can't help screaming in pain. Now it's out from under the bin I will be able to get out of this, but first I will have to make a splint for my leg.

This splint is made from crap from the bin. There is a small piece of metal that I am using with a piece of bent plastic that fits perfectly around my knee. I put the metal through my shoe and twist it into the plastic. When twisting, the pain courses through by stiff body. I only just stifle a scream. The station seems eerie; I can hear a pin drop.

I see that all the doors are boarded up with rotting wood; this might be my way out! I break down the barrier and fall through. I hit my head on the wall. Now I remember why my dad died. He had cancer. But that's not the reason he died; the reason is because I didn't pay for his cancer treatment as I was sure he would survive on his own. But the cancer got bad and when he died he never blamed me; he knew I was doing what I thought was right. It was the wrong decision.

I wake up, but this time on the other side of the door. I have finally done it. I'm out. Then I realise I'm not. I'm dismayed. Suddenly, out of the corner of my eye I see something familiar, and I realise it's me…

I see myself tie the splint to my leg and it dawns on me that I'm in a loop. Suddenly a great sadness overcomes me, thinking that my father died, how much I miss him, and now I'm stuck in this loop.

A train comes, and I feel incredibly happy – I might be saved. But the train carries on past me.

Hours pass and I think to myself, next time a train comes I'll throw myself in front of it…there is no point living inside a loop.

Then I see a light from the subway tracks. The train comes and my instincts don't stop me. I want to join my father. I throw myself in front of the train.

A jolt wakes me, and a hospital nurse tells me to stay calm and tells me I'm in hospital and I was shot! By my brother.

KENNING POEMS

BY TALIA

As the mysteriously-dark corner taunted me,

Echoes of silence filled the air

I saw something tiptoe in front of my door,

Before scaring me into an abyss of darkness

I screamed and screamed,

But nothing answered me,

I cried and wailed,

Until I realised I'd failed.

I fell and hit the ground,

A thick floor-blinder swirled around,

A nightmare-creator, a sweet dream-haunter

Jumped out and finished its job

BY WiLL

The white-glare casts an eerie light over the dark forest

The wet-cloud hides the secrets of the wood

The forest-creatures don't show themselves

The water bubbles through the rocks

BY EViE

The floor-blanket withers in the atmosphere

Where humanly-canines lurk

And the echoing silence engulfs me.

The scattering of the ravenous-rodents

Break the sound of the dull-blankness

SHINE ON THE BLOOD
RiLEY MILLS

I'm walking to Chantelle's house. It's in eye view now, quite dark;
the waves crashing into the rocks is ear-stabbingly loud. Lights are
on but nobody is home. I approach the front door, but I feel like
someone's watching me. I don't wait to turn around – I can feel icy
breath down my neck, sending shivers down my spine. My only
instinct is to run for my life. I think I'll lose them on the beach.
I might have a shot of survival hiding in the cracks of the beach's
hideouts. I try to find a gap – none…*what do I do?* I can feel a
warm tear run down my face, and another … then a continuous
flow. The moment I've been dreading is here. I feel my body hit the
floor, my head pounding, then suddenly, nothing. I can't even feel a
presence in my body.

* * *

"Come on Jen, we've got to hide the body – there's no tea and coffee in prison. Hurry up!" shouts Chantelle.

"Shoot, it's Jonathan," says Jennifer.

Jonathan's seen Edward's body and is flabbergasted at the sight. He asks what's happened and the two girls act like they're clueless in the situation.

"Chantelle it was you!" exclaims Jonathan.

"What are you on about?" she shouts back.

"Give it up, Chan, he knows," says Jennifer.

"Your sequin's on his blood right there, it has to be you," he shouts.

Jonathan runs off to call the police.

"There's no point chasing him. I'll take the blame Jennifer, my fault. You don't want to go down with me. Now run, please," sighs Chantelle.

"I'll avenge you – I promise they'll all get what they deserve, I tell you that now," Jennifer distantly shouts.

The police sirens start getting closer. Chantelle slowly steps back with her blood-covered hands up in the air.

Ed is left on the floor, crying out to anyone who's around … he's gonna bleed out to death if nobody comes to save him. Chantelle is running toward him, dodging plants and tangles faster than an Olympian. She kneels down in front of Ed.

Suddenly, a figure emerges from behind. It's Jennifer, holding the same blood-soaked knife she impaled Ed with. Jennifer swings her knife, slicing open Chantelle's head, not realising that she has just murdered her own daughter. Jennifer is running away, passing clueless Jonathan. He's still trying to work out the map system of the graveyard.

The beasts of the police are howling, chasing, and spreading terror onto Jen's face. She sees no way out but there's one option … it's not rational or safe but most definitely a way out of this pursuit. Jennifer sprints to the end of the pier and leaps off. Her back smashes against the hard soaked rocks. Every bone snaps and just like all her victims, Jennifer is dead.

*   *   *

It's been a month now, and Jonathan is still being questioned about what he knows of Jennifer's, Ed's, and Edward's death. He's now all alone and scared of the thought that there is the slightest chance that Jennifer is alive and coming for him. After all, her body was never found…

HELL'S HOUSE
BY CHANDLER GUMBRILL

"Come on," cried Jennifer.

The house sat there on the edge of the woodland. Ed climbed out of the van; the other three were already making their way to the house. The house looked dead – it hadn't been inhabited since 1917. It was now 1961. Upon entry it was dusty, cold, and empty. Dust started to collect on Jennifer's black dress. Chantelle started to look around the bleak house. She was wearing a beaded dress. Ed, who was wearing a T-shirt and jeans, entered the building. Piercing echoes of silence roared in his ears.

"Hello," shouted Ed.

"Ed!" cried back a voice. It was John.

"Look, our van is broken so we're gonna have to stay the night," cried Ed.

John wandered to a table in what looked to be a living room. It had a newspaper on it. 'The Scranton Times.' It read:

....

SCRANTON TIMES

Four dead in old farmhouse mass murder!

....

John realised they had made a mistake to stop there. Soon the day became night. The four friends each had a room. Ed was just washing up from dinner. John realised that dinner had been an hour ago, so he went to see Ed.

"Ed!"

John was shocked at what he saw.

There was a pile of mucky old plates in the sink and lying on the floor in a pool of his own blood was Ed, with a brick in his hand.

"Shoot John," cried Jennifer.

"What did you do?" cried Chantelle.

Chantelle walked over to Jennifer.

"I thought you hid the body," she whispered.

"Didn't have time," Jennifer whispered back.

"Then we will have to kill John," cried Chantelle.

John was already making his way through the house to his room He heard the creaking on the stairs.

"John, we just want to talk," cried Chantelle.

John turned the doorknob to lock the door. Chantelle was already racing to his door.

"Come on, open up John, I love you," shouted Chantelle.

The door started to shake with the doorknob rattling.

"You and Jennifer are murderers!" John cried.

The only thing in the room was a bed and an old blue phone. John took the phone, shaking

"Get the axe Jen," Chantelle shouted.

Then there was silence while John called the police. A crackling voice answered.

"Hello? 999, what's your emergency?" the voice said.

The door smashed pieces of wood everywhere. Jennifer stood there smiling, with bulging green eyes.

"It was me John, me! Chantelle is far gone now so I'm going to take the blame."

Jennifer laughed after saying this.

"Hi, I'd like to report a murder!" John screamed down the phone.

IS THIS THE END?
BY JADE JOY

There's a murder at a seaside. A small town close to the sea. The police have been trying to pin this murderer for three years and now he's struck again. An 18-year-old girl, her father close by, down a dark path late at night. The girl's father sees the murderer run off; he quickly takes a picture of him on his phone as he slips out of sight, the quick camera flash in the dark blinding his sight, reflecting the light off the killer's knife.

Two weeks after his daughter's death, he keeps looking back at the picture of an average night, blurred figure wearing black hoodie and joggers, a black mask covering his identity. He hasn't slept properly for days; he blames himself. Every time he tries to sleep the gutting image of his daughter's lifeless body laid out in front of him, fills his blank mind.

He's tired, heartbroken. She was all he had. His wife had died in a car accident when his daughter was just six years old. He is frustrated, he wants to find this person and stab them to death. He is filled with rage. He can't just leave this killer running in the streets.

He wishes he saw the killer's face. He can't stand this; he needs to find this person and kill them. He thinks to himself, this is insane, I can't find this person.

But he wants to try, he wants to stab this person till there is nothing left but a chopped-up corpse covering the street.

* * *

It's been five weeks since his daughter's death. His phone is endlessly ringing, calls from school asking where she is, calls from his mother questioning why she can't come over to visit. He decides to take a stroll through town to try to clear his mind, find a dark alleyway to squash down the obsessive urge to find this person and end them.

He finds a dark alleyway, but it's not empty. There's an average-sized figure wearing a black hoodie and joggers: the same black masked face, the same knife in their hand. He digs deep into his pocket for his phone, flicking through pictures, desperately trying to find that one image. He finds it. It's a match: the same knife handle, the same mask, the same everything. It's as if the chance has come to him.

The figure hasn't seen him standing watching down the end of the alleyway. The killer looks away. This is his chance – he runs for the knife, feeling the damp walls of the alleyway get narrower. He hasn't been seen …. *is he really there? Am I imagining it all?* He doesn't stop, he runs, he's almost there. He grabs the knife from the killer's hand and stabs the black figure in the back before he has a chance to turn around.

A feeling of guilt and relief at the same time rains over him, weighing his shoulders down.

The masked figure falls to the floor. He falls to his knees, not knowing what to do next. *I just killed someone.* That's all he can see in his blurred mind.

He stands up, looking down at the body by his feet. He gathers his thoughts. *So, who killed my daughter?* He pulls the mask off the dead corpse, only to reveal a very familiar face. His brother.

Now what? I can't just leave my brother's lifeless body in an empty street. He picks up the body, every part of him filling with regret. His house is close, across the street and up the private road. He walks with the mangled body hanging over his shoulder – he's reached the private road now. He hasn't seen anyone. He couldn't explain himself if he did.

He gets to the house and empties out his large work bag, stuffing the body, knife, and his phone in the bag. He stumbles out to his garden in his confusion, and grabs a few bricks, stuffing them into the bag too. He struggles but manages to haul the bag into the boot of his car.

He drives down to the overgrown river that no one ever goes to, apart from the fisherman.

"No one will find him," he says to himself, voice trembling.

He parks close to the path, opening the boot of his car, wondering if he should really be doing this. What else would he do? He throws in the bag, watching it sink down to the riverbed.
Is this the end?

*   *   *

The body has stayed weighed down in the river for two weeks now. He's convinced that he's got away with murder. He hasn't left the house since: guilt fills his gut. He's decided to try to overcome the guilt. He walks down to the river in the evening breeze, sun setting. He reaches the river, the sun shining over the water. He stands dead still across from the river on the empty concrete path, eyes wide, expression shocked and frozen. He is looking at the bag that he put the body in…ripped open and hooked on a branch up the riverbank with nothing but two bricks in…no body. As the sunlight fades away, in the distance something is floating down the river.

ESCAPE
BY FREYA PURDIE

Rick couldn't believe that he had ended up hiding in an abandoned hospital. He hated hospitals. He hadn't been near one since his wife died in childbirth. At that moment he was hiding from a bunch of men who wanted to shoot him. He gathered that they were very annoyed because he killed one of their men.

Turning round the corner Rick went into a room, closed the door, and slid down it. Looking around the room his eyes drifted across the many shards of glass shattered on the ground. There was a surgical bed set up in the middle of the room. It was covered in dirt and smelt like burning paper. The walls were a faded shade of sky blue. There was a battered metal circle with a hole in it, which was hanging above the bed.

While he was staring mindlessly at the room, the sudden sound of footsteps drew closer. Rick sucked in a breath as several of them passed the door. After about a minute their steps got quieter. Rick let out the breath he was holding, starting to get up. Then the handle of the door started to move.

Rick started to panic. There wasn't anywhere to go. Just as he was about to give up, he spotted a slight crack in the wall. It was another door. He quickly rushed over there, steadily avoiding shards of glass that littered the floor. Slowly he opened the door to the hallway. Carefully he slipped through just as the men entered the room. He tried to slink away but of course something had to go wrong – one of the men. They stared at each other for a while before he shouted, "Guys, he's here!"

Rick thought it was a good idea to start running now. He darted down the hall when he heard a gunshot and then an indescribable pain erupted in his left leg. He'd been shot. He turned to the left and headed for the closest door, hoping that there was a lock on the door. Sadly, there wasn't. It was slightly hidden on the outside. He kept note of it just in case he could use it to help himself escape.

He suddenly remembered his leg and started to roll up his jeans. It seemed the bullet had only grazed his leg, which was a good sign. He needed to act quickly, or it was going to be a very painful death for him. Scanning around the room, he started searching for anything he could use as a weapon. He noticed a wooden bat leaning against the wall in front of him. Before he could get it he needed to block the door, just for a moment. As he started to hear the thundering footsteps he leapt towards a wooden chair, grabbed it, and shoved it under the door handle. He quickly grabbed the bat and waited for the handle to start twisting. He readied himself.

He heard the rotten wood crack, and he knew he had to be fast. The men flooded in baring their weapons. One of them rushed forward. Rick swung the bat into the middle of his face. He heard the bones in the man's nose crack. Rick winced. He tumbled towards Rick. Rick leaned to the left. The man crashed into the wall and then he fell through.

As the door that the man fell on flung open, a cloud of dust lifted into the air, distracting the other men. Rick darted out of the room and slammed the door shut, hoping that there was another lock on the outside. There was. He locked it and ran, nearly tripping over the body on the ground.

He sprinted down the corridor and round to the dust-filled room.

"Idiots," he mumbled, and slammed the door, locking it like he did the other one.

Rick stepped back, sighing. He flinched when a loud bang sounded on the door. Rick smirked and jogged off, searching for a map of the hospital he saw when he was running by.

After five minutes he found it. Following the map's directions, he found the way out. As he stepped outside he squinted at the glare of the sunlight. He glanced around, spotting a vehicle that he assumed was the men's. He hobbled over and peered into the window. The keys were still hanging in the ignition. Rick opened the door and climbed in. He sunk into the comfortable seat, exhausted.

After a while he started up the car and pulled out of the hospital. When he had covered some distance, Rick wondered why he was even in that hospital in the first place. He thought it was because that was the only place he could go at the time, but Rick thought about it for a moment and came to the conclusion that the only reason he went in there was because he missed his long dead wife and thought it would remind him of her.

Rick smiled as he felt a large weight lifted off his shoulders.

TRUTHS AND SECRETS
BY TALIA STUDLEY

I went to bed after my argument with grandfather. I didn't understand why no one would tell me the truth about my dad. Mother's been close to telling me many times before, and if it wasn't for grandfather, maybe she would have done so already.

Oh, wait! My dad had a mate in the war. He told me so in his letters. If I could remember his name ... he was Irish, liked whiskey. I got it! Shamrock. He lives somewhere in the woods. I'll find him. I gently drifted off, my chaos of thoughts getting quieter. I slept.

I woke up. I was drowsy and my room was cold. I put my hand out on the cold floor ... what? I woke up fully with a start. I wasn't in my room. I didn't know where I was. I jumped up and tried to get away when suddenly the chain attached to my ankle jerked.

"No. No. Nooo!" I screamed.

At that point I was crying.

"No," I choked.

"Shut up with your whining!"

My grandfather shambled in, two men armed with bows and arrows behind.

"Where am I? What have you done?" I yelled, standing up. "You monster. What have you done?" I shouted.

Grandfather clicked his fingers and the next thing I knew I was in a heap on the floor with an arrow in my leg. I ripped it out and threw it across the floor.

"You're a monster," I sobbed.

"No, I'm loyal and don't force people to tell me things that don't concern me," Grandfather said sneerily. "At least I don't run around and act like the whole world revolves around me."

"Yea, well at least I don't act like you and threaten people as if they're slaves," I shot back. "I will find a way." My confidence was rising.

"Yeah well, good luck getting out of here."

The three of them left and I searched for a way out. After four hours of rummaging, I found a key to the chain. It was under a loose rock in the wall. My leg throbbed. The best I could do was a rag. I took off the chain and grabbed a rock and smashed the window. Jumping out, I headed to the woods.

I stumbled into the woods: further, faster. My leg was throbbing from the arrow and my vision was getting fuzzy. I came across some giant leaves, so I decided I'd wrap up my wound. I grabbed two and tied the stems together before I wrapped the leaves around my leg. I spotted a vine hanging off a tree and broke off a bit of that to tie the leaves' tips. The leaves were cool and damp, and I was grateful. I carried on for what seemed like hours when I eventually came across an abandoned theme park. I limped past several bumper cars with chipped paint. I glanced down at my clothes; my shorts were tatty and faded and my t-shirt was ripped. I sighed. I stared at my boots. There was dried mud caked on them with another fresh layer splattered on. That was just adding insult to injury. All of a sudden, I heard a twig snap.

"Well, this is just outrageous!" a deep voice taunted.

I recognised that voice. That voice could be the end of me. I heard a gun click, and then…

I'd been discovered. I sighed. Most likely grandfather again. I turned around and walked to stand in the doorway. I was right. I stood in the doorway to stare at my grandfather yet again, still armed with his WWII gun.

"How many times have I told you, girl? When will you get it into your head that no one cares about your dad and will not tell you the truth?"

"You are much mistaken, old man," my mother's familiar voice exclaimed.

She ran up to me and stood in front of me, blocking my path.

"You stupid woman. You should've stayed at home."

"Why would I do that when my daughter's life is in danger?"

There were tears in her voice as she held her ground.

"Get out of the way Lynette. Move over or I'll shoot you like I did your sister and brother."

Grandfather's voice was harsh and taunting, and mum was beginning to shake. Grandfather sniggered deviously.

"Go on, move," he said. "MOVE!"

"No. I will not stop at anything. Especially if my daughter's involved. "

"Well, it's her fault it's your funeral," grandfather boomed.

BANG!

"Noooo!" I screamed.

I had to leave my dead mother behind and run as fast as I could. After a long trip, I came to Shamrock's home. I stumbled up to the door and knocked. A tall man with a wooden cane answered.

"Yes?" he said, in a slow, deep voice.

"I'm Talia Young," I said, breathlessly, "Can you tell me what really happened to my father?"

* * *

Shamrock poured us a small glass of whiskey and sat down.

"Well?" I said, preparing myself.

"Right. It was near the end of the war and there was a shell aimed directly at me. Apart from fighting on different sides, me and your father weren't that different. So, your father saw and saved me. Your grandfather was so against this and he …" Shamrock breathed slowly. "Your grandfather shot him."

I gasped. My hand shook.

"I'm sorry," Shamrock said, sadly.

*   *   *

I left sadly, wondering if this was really worth it. I felt Shamrock watch me as I left, with my injured leg throbbing. I wandered home in sadness. As I walked through the door, grandfather was on the stairs.

"Found out, did you? Regret asking, do you?" he asked drearily. It was obvious he'd been drinking.

"Can I have some alcohol?" I asked, not expecting much. Even being drunk, he could still use his brain.

"Yea, help yourself. Not gonna do you much good though."

Grandfather made his way upstairs.

"Thanks," I mumbled, making my way to the basement.

Once I got there I searched for the Glenfiddich and drank the whole bottle. Then, feeling a bit lightheaded, I found Jack Daniels and drank two bottles. I crawled along the cold stone floor until I found strong tequila. I only managed half a bottle before I passed out.

The Grandfather

Stupid girl. I wasn't that drunk, but I hadn't expected to find her passed out after three and a half hours of excessive drinking. She'd been on the strong, expensive stuff. I thought she'd have a glass or two of wine or something, not throw back tequila and whiskey.

I took her to the hospital and explained what happened. She was taken to the room and wired up to things. I didn't really know what was going on. She was an alcoholic, just like her father. I stayed until she woke up, which wasn't until the next day.

"Sober?" I asked.

"What? I don't…where am…what happened?"

"Well, thing is, you're an alcoholic. You drank three and a half bottles of strong stuff, then you passed out. Now you're in hospital."

"Wow. I didn't think this would happen. I'm sorry."

"No, it's ok. Not like I'm ever seeing you again."

I pulled a bomb out of my pocket.

"Fifteen minutes, then you're gonna go boom."

I fixed it to the bottom of the bed.

"Bye bye…forever."

I left, grinning like a cat. I thought I saw someone familiar, but I ignored it.

Talia

I was shocked. He was a murderer. Just then, Shamrock came around the corner with his phone.

"Are you ok?" he asked.

"Not really. I'm an alcoholic and my grandfather's a murderer."

"Aye, that he is," Shamrock agreed. "I got a video; I'm going to the police."

And with that, he was gone. I was just left to wonder.

An hour or so later, the bomb squad had been, and I'd been questioned by the police. So had my grandfather, and he was a prisoner for the rest of his short, miserable life. Good riddance.

Four years later

I'm now 19 years old and I live with Shamrock in the woods. I got therapy for my drinking, and I've been sober ever since. My grandfather died. I've learned more about my dad and wrote a book. If you're wondering what it's about, you already know; you just finished reading it!

THE SPIRIT
BY SUMMER DONOGHUE

There was no door. I don't know how I got there but it seemed
familiar. As soon as I stepped in the house I could feel something
bad happened here. In front of me was a once-grand staircase.
I started to climb the steps, the sound of my footsteps echoing.
When I reached the top of the stairs, there were three doors in
front of me. *How was I meant to know which one to go in?* It could
be my only chance. But once again I somehow knew which one to
go in: the left-hand one. My feet started to move slowly towards
the door. Six feet from it. Four feet from it. Two feet from it. Just
as I reached for the door handle I heard it again. The hiss of wind
that called my name, "Jesss, Jesss."

As suddenly as it came, the hiss went. I turned back to the door,
and it was open. Funny, I didn't think I opened it yet, but I must
have. Shrugging this off, I walked confidently into the room. As

soon as I reached the centre, I was sure. This was it. This was where it happened. This was where I was knocked unconscious and put in a coma for two months. I wanted to know why. *What was I doing here?* This ends here. It had gone far enough.

I shut the door and returned to the centre of the room. It happened, I felt it. Spinning on the spot, my pulse quickened. But nothing was there. No. I thought this would work. Then it happened.

A piercing scream filled the air. Where was this coming from? Covering my ears, I tried to search for the source of the sound. The screaming stopped, leaving a ringing in its place. I heard the squeak of rusty metal. I turned slowly on the spot. On the bed was a person. Were they a person? It looked slightly misty and transparent.

"Who are you?" I asked, softly.

"Something you will never know," came a gravelly voice.

"Are you a ghost? I need to know."

"Jesss."

Another hiss.

"No, I am a spirit," the spirit said calmly.

My breath had become uneven and rapid.

"Why?"

"Because I need to tell you something, something very important that will change your life forever."

"Tell me here. Tell me right here, right now."

My voice was growing louder and louder with every word.

"You want to know what happened the day you were found unconscious, you want to know why everything is going your way?"

"Yes, tell me. I am dying to know. "

The spirit didn't answer. He just looked at me.

"Jess, this isn't real. It's happening in your brain … you're still in a coma," he added softly.

I spluttered that this couldn't be true. I started to speak but a tremendous bang stopped me. Suddenly the spirit looked frightened. The spirit jumped off the bed and ran forward.

"Jess, listen to me very carefully. You have the power to go back, not the choice to go forward."

"Death," he added to my questioning look.

"Death is coming here to take you. If you want to go back, to live, you have to go now," he whispered urgently.

"How do I go back?" I breathed.

"Think of the happiest memory you can – a reason for you to go back."

Silence filled the room. One memory came to mind. It was the day my dad returned home. He had been injured in action. But after he recovered he flew home from the army to meet me. That was the best day of my life.

I snapped back to reality.

"Have you got it?" the spirit asked.

"Yes."

"Ok, you have to be quick with this…very quick. Death is on their way."

Just as the spirit finished a darkness spread through the room. The spirit gasped and ran to the door. Then the hissing started again, only this time it was constant. *Was I going mad?* The spirit called through the black mist that was growing ever darker.

"Now Jess, do it now. I don't know how long I can hold them off for."

I turned my mind to my dad and all the feelings I felt on that day come rushing back to me Then I saw him: my dad walking in the airport. I remember running as fast as I could to him. A tremendous bang filled the room, and everything went black.

The fluorescent light stung my eyes.

"Jess? Oh my god, Jess?"

My dad threw himself on me and burst into tears.

"Dad? Come on dad, I'm ok. Pull yourself together."

"Sorry Jess, but I thought I was going to lose you!" my dad cried.

The doctors came in and told me what had happened. I had been hit on the head with a brick when the old mansion that me and my friends were in, collapsed. I had been out for two months. After the doctors left, I looked out of the window and saw the first daffodil bloom.

A HERO'S JOURNEY
BY DANNY PARKINSON

Two men were ordered to get in a ship; it looked like a tin. It was approximately 11:15pm when they left France, now it was 06:44am, when they heard gunshots whizzing past their ships. You could see the bang of the machine gun bullets hitting the boats, nervous men heading to the rough sand in their heavy metal boats.

Finally, the first boat opened. The men charged, the machine guns ripping through their flesh, the soldiers falling with a thud. The soldiers got more nervous seeing their colleagues die, but they knew they needed to win for their country.

Max's boat opened – Max was using dead corpses as his advantage to get to the side of the mountains so he could sneak attack the Germans. A man called Kenny joined him on the quest; they were heading to a silent village but then a bullet whizzed past them.

They were wrong. The Germans were hiding in the village; they were surrounded. The Germans locked Max and Kenny in a house.

They thought that was the last of them, but Kenny remembered he had a pistol in his pocket. He used the pistol to break a window and run for it. They ran through the village until Max got a stitch, and a German shot his leg, ripping right through his flesh. Max thought he was done for until Kenny saw the German and shot him. Kenny saw Max's trousers soak up the blood and knew that if he didn't act fast, his comrade would die. So, Kenny ripped part of Max's trousers and used it as a bandage to wrap the wound. He carried Max to a house to give him some treatment, because in Kenny's past he was a medical expert before he was a soldier. Now he was using his medical school expertise to his advantage, to save a man's life.

Kenny found a walking stick in the house and gave it to Max so he could walk better until he got better treatment. They were back on track. They walked to the forest, getting closer to one of the German camps without knowing, but they heard some people speaking German. Kenny told Max to put mud on himself as camouflage so the Germans couldn't see him. They used the camouflage and stabbed the Germans stealthily one by one, until the camp was silent.

They walked into the first tent with caution. It was full of guns and ammo. Max took a M16, and Kenny took a M1 Garand, walked to the ammo, and took a handful. They quickly threw it into their bags, trying to be as silent as possible. They sneaked to the next tent where they saw lots of atomic bombs and mustard gas. They were shocked at this discovery. They took some mustard gas and ran to the last tent. There was a picture of a German's family and there was German writing that translated, 'Why did I have to be forced to fight in this stupid war? It's suicide.'

Max and Kenny looked at each other. They walked out of the tent with tears in their eyes, but they carried on walking to the forest and shot any German in their way until they found another camp, because they had to do it to win. They walked into the camp and threw mustard gas into all of the tents and waited for the Germans to run out so Kenny could shoot them one by one. The blinded men ran out of their tents only to get a bullet ripping and crushing their skulls. One by one they fell with a thud.

Finally, the mustard gas cleared, and Max and Kenny entered the tent looking for the map to the capital; they knew it was there. They looked in each tent and finally found the map and followed it to the capital. They spent hours in the forests until they found it.

They hid behind a broken-down building and were trying to find a better route to the house where Hitler was hiding. They found a jeep and sneakily hopped into the back. Then the jeep started moving. After what seemed like an hour Hitler then made an announcement warning everyone that there were French in the city.

"You must find them," he demanded.

Max jumped out of the jeep in the capital.

"Come out and fight me Hitler," he demanded, banging on the door of Hitler's house.

Hitler walked out and shot Max in the pelvis. He felt the pain sear through his body, but Max slipped the M1 Garand into Hitler's pocket, such was his passion to kill the tyrant. Hitler didn't know. Then the time struck as Hitler walked back into his house.

BOOM!

Hitler exploded and the Germans were confused. Kenny helped Max, then the French and British arrived. They were surprised at the turn of events.

* * *

Max got treatment and a medal for being a hero, and Kenny got a promotion to General Marksman. Finally, Kenny had the urge to ask Max out. Max thought for a while and finally said yes, and kissed his comrade. They had the rest of their lives together after they retired, after they defeated Hitler, and Kenny took Max on a date to a fancy restaurant.

KENNING POEMS

BY EVIE

Her bloodshot sight-givers

Her chipped food-chewers

Her bloody scent-giver

Her distorted all sorts

All give me terrifying-thoughts

At my time of rest.

BY RILEY

As the fright-bringer comes along, the grey-blindfold isn't far

behind and the black-clay rises up above, then the taunting

tension creeps up on you.

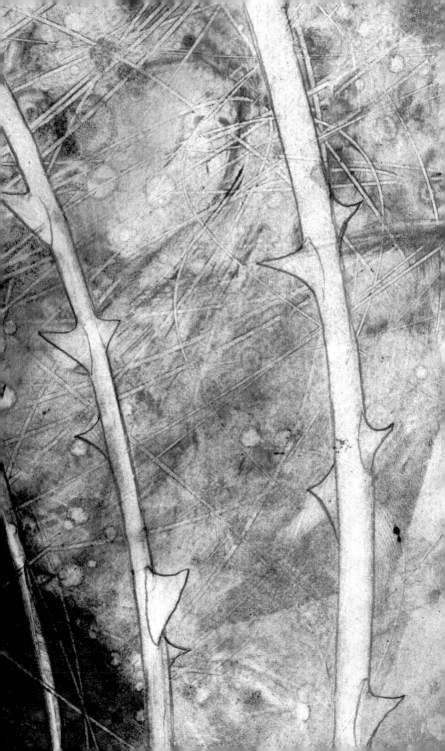

ECHOES OF SILENCE
BY ZOE STAAL

Trisha Nord was like any ordinary student, studying philosophy at university near to her home in the lovely and secluded village of Fimble in England. The village was ancient and mysterious. Everyone living there stood upon grounds of bloodshed, a coastal village built by settlers from 400-360 BC. At the dawn of dusk the entire village altered. As if entering a different reality. Feeding off the mysterious echoes of silence. Shadows of mist emerged beneath the Fall Cliffs, from the dark and shady forest full of wonders and history. It was a wonderous tourist attraction for many people visiting the sizeable village. They would be out of their minds to want to visit it for any other reason.

Trisha Nord was hardly the nicest of people to walk the planet. She never seemed to have a clear head. She treated the people that she met terribly. With 12 separate romantic relationships since she moved to Fimble in order to continue her studies and achieve a bachelor's degree, all of those relationships ended on bad terms.

Late at midnight on the 24th of November 2014, Trisha was sleeping in her old and tattered student accommodation when she woke up in her car. Sitting in the passenger seat of her car, parked in an old and dilapidated eight-storey car park, with echoes ringing through her ears. Voices repeatedly screaming "Leave here! Leave here!"

However, she was drawn into it like a moth is drawn to a flame in the depths of night. A mist surrounded the bottom of the car and promptly dispersed as she hesitantly opened the door. The floor was cold and dimly lit as Trisha took a step onto the dark concrete floor. The lights looming and flickering above her head had scrambled from cars passing through. However, it was evident that cars had not driven through there for a very long time. The sound of water fiercely gushing through pipes, clattering many storeys up, was a clearly audible cacophony. In the far corner of her eyes, Trisha saw the old and rusted steel doors. Glistening, beckoning her to come over. Apprehensively, Trisha trekked across the concrete floor. The top of her every footstep bounced off the walls and rang ear splittingly in her ears. Upon her approach to the elevator doors, they slid open slowly and she froze. Stopped dead in her tracks. The faint 'ding' of the elevator rang through the car park as the elevator doors made a jolt and came to a halt.

Standing on the iron plate at the centre of the floor of the elevator compartment was a grey, shadowy figure. It emitted a cloudy mist that lingered with the scent of burning wood and brick. As the mist poured out of the elevator and rose through the ceiling, the figure took a mere three steps before Trisha began to turn around and sprint for her life. She didn't look back; all she did was run. All that flooded her mind was making it to safety. As she sprinted for her car, it seemed as if the distance between her and it was getting wider and wider. The walls were stretching outwards. More shadowy figures appeared. Two, three, four….12. The car was just an arm's reach away when they pounced on her, the floor gave way beneath her feet, and she slipped away into darkness.

Trisha sat up immediately in her bed breathing heavily, terrified. It was raining heavily outside. The raindrops tapped on her window and thunder sounded in the cloudy sky. She still heard the same voices cackling in and out of her ears. As she pulled herself out of her bed, pulling away the freezing cold duvet, she heard the kettle inside the kitchen hissing. She ran in to see water boiling. *How?* she thought to herself, astounded. Trisha walked over and poured herself a mug of tea. She sat at the table sipping away at it through the night, thinking about what had happened. Her mind was still roving.

Trisha continued to think, even when she made her way to lectures and classes during the day. Thoughts began to glaze across her mind, thinking that maybe somebody was punishing her for everything that had happened. The thoughts and emotions overwhelmed her. *What can I do?! How!* she thought. Trisha jumped out of her seat and ran out of the lecture hall, crying.

As she took a long and panicked walkthrough the park, she began to remember everything that she had done. The threatening her partners, the verbal abuse, everything.

Trisha began to regret. She thought that perhaps there was a way to make amends for how she had treated people. As if it had been planted into her mind, she recognised the exact place from her dream. She decided that to escape from her thoughts, she had to go back there.

Before long, she was in her car driving. Further and further. She had no idea how, but Trisha knew exactly where she was headed. After 50 minutes of constant driving, she arrived at a dark concrete structure, filled with overgrown ivy and garbage. She caught a glimpse of a sign diverting her inside; she proceeded onwards.

The building was precisely identical to the one from her dream. On the very bottom floor the walls and pillars were covered in notes. Everywhere, on every wall and every pillar. She turned off her car and got out quickly. She ran to a wall and read one of the notes.

'There is no escaping this.'

She ran to another.

'You did this to us!'

And finally, in the middle of the floor, was a note. The note read:

'If you ever want this to stop, burn down the church and come to the peak of the Fall Cliff.'

Trisha stood there in total shock and astonishment. She knew she had to do as the note instructed. She was desperate.

Trisha drove down the same long and arduous route back to Fimble and parked at the church. Waiting for her was a can of gasoline and a lighter. She got out of her car once again. Desperation overwhelmed her. She walked in and poured the flammable liquid on the floor and lit it up. Walking out of the church, her car had disappeared. She didn't care anymore. Feeling numb, she began the walk to the Fall Cliff.

The voices still rang in her ears. The piercing screams.

As she reached the mountain edge, she picked up another note.

'It is over now.'

As she read these words, her heart sank and she felt the dagger pierce through her skull.

Trisha Nord collapsed, plummeting to her death.

After the long night of her body lying in the sand, the police arrived.

"So, Trisha Nord is her name. 5'10", female, 17. A student at Colecan college."

"Wow, I'm dumbfounded. Must have been a pretty difficult and distressing death," said the coroner.

"Any information regarding the status of the death? Murder or suicide?" replied the officer, while slowly making their way through an éclair.

"Not yet. However, by the end of the day we will have a full report. There are signs of a severe trauma wound to the head and torso, as well as a stab wound through the centre of the skull," the coroner continued gravely.

"I would fairly confidently say that they were chucked off that cliff to the east and washed up at shore," the officer exclaimed.

"What's that tattoo?" asked the coroner.

"I don't know. Do you think it means anything? It's just lines."

The coroner continued, "This could be evidence. Bag up the body and get it into the van."

"Yes doc," replied the officer.

The coroner looked irritated.

"Don't call me that."

They picked up the stretcher with the body bag placed upon it and solemnly walked back up the hill, leaving the beach.

It was later discovered that there was never a murder at all. Ghosts of Trisha's past were responsible for the death. But nobody would ever know that it was anything other than a suicide. Fimble was never the same again.

TWISTED
BY KATIE GREEN

He was the fittest guy in school. Jealousy levels were high, someone wanted to destroy Ben's life. Ben thought it would be an ordinary date, but he was wrong. He had walked into a death-trap.

* * *

I woke up on a rusty, old bed. The smell of disinfectant was super strong. A strong sense of nausea hit me. I slowly sat up, looking around. *Where was I?* As I studied my surroundings I started to remember. I was meeting up with a girl I had met online; she told me to meet her here. The place must have been an old hospital. An old theatre lamp was hanging off the ceiling, glass littering the floor like a carpet. *But where was Becky?*

As I called out, I heard a door bang and the crunch of glass. I called out again, but no reply. I slid off the bed, treading carefully around the shards of broken glass. I stepped out into a dark corridor, looking around. It was so dark even though it was about midday. There were not many windows in this place.

I turned into yet another room and there seemed to be light coming out of the wall, but there wasn't a window there. I stumbled over the destroyed door frame to take a closer look. As I walked around I saw something on the chair. There was something on there, covered up with a piece of fabric. Slowly and carefully, I lifted up the cloth.

Underneath it was a doll.

A doll that looked like me.

I took one look at it and threw it away from me as hard as I could. It hit the wall with a loud, satisfying thud.

"Aarghh."

My shoulder was excruciatingly painful. It was like whatever happened to the doll, happened to me.

Suddenly, a dark thing dropped from the ceiling…

The figure stood tall. An inch or two taller than me. I jumped, instantly ready to fight.

"Who are you?"

I could hear the fear in my own voice. The cloaked figure took a small step forward and removed the balaclava that was shielding its face. I stared in surprise.

"Yo, Tyler. Whatcha doing here?"

"Did you find Becky?" Tyler asked sarcastically.

I flinched as though he'd slapped me.

"Wait, hang on. How did you know?"

Tyler walked to the wall where the voodoo doll lay.

"Well. I guess you must know," he said.

"What have you done to Becky?" I was shouting.

Tyler just laughed.

"Oh, I've done nothing to Becky."

He paused.

"I am Becky."

Tyler now started to turn towards the doll. I just stood there, confused and angry. Tyler picked up the doll. I sprang into action as Tyler fumbled to get a needle out of his pocket. I tried to grab the doll when Tyler's fist connected with my gut, sending me stumbling backwards, the air knocked out of me. I punched Tyler's jaw, surprising him, making his grip loose on the needle. I seized the needle and launched it into the dark corridor.

Both of us were now glaring at each other trying to decide whether to punch each other again, whether to carry on fighting. I turned around.

"Enough. Why are you doing this, Tyler? What have I done to you?"

Tyler laughed.

"You have it all easy. You are perfect. Why can't you ever do anything wrong? Literally everyone is in love with you. Every person sings your praises. You have good grades and you don't even study. That's why I'm doing this."

I stared, open-mouthed.

"Tyler my life ain't perfect, far from it. And what do you mean? I do study when there's a test coming up. I just can't believe you went to the extreme to get at me. I still cannot believe you pretended to like me, and that you were a girl. YOU TOLD ME YOU LOVED ME. You were Becky and I hate you for that."

Tyler looked down, face chalky-white.

"Ben," Tyler's voice cracked with emotion, "Ben, I wasn't pretending…"

My eyes widened with shock.

"Ben, I like you."

I went a pasty-white colour, unsure how to feel.

"Um, great. Sorry to be blunt, but how to we get out of here?"

Tyler blushed crimson red.

"The window, there."

I reached out for the window, pulling myself up and out. When I was out, I turned and smiled at Tyler, holding out my hand.

"You coming?"

Tyler grinned, taking my hand. When we were both out, our hands hadn't disconnected; our fingers stayed entwined.

THE FALL
BY EVIE BAKER

An angel. Yes, an angel. An angel who had fallen from heaven. Landing in the depths of a deep, dark forest. Thankfully she landed in a pile of hay, embracing her. No injuries, except a deep cut across her forehead. Her feathers were muffled, and her hair was matted with hay and blood. The towering trees loomed over her presence, forbidding any light to pass through. The forest stretched for miles in every direction.

You may think, why would an angel be in a setting like this? Well, she was thrown down to earth for her own safety. Who threw her? Her parents. In order to protect her from being pierced by the devil, her parents sent her to this atmosphere, and they were executed shortly after. She was yet to know where she was. She was yet to know that she was lost within this dark place called Earth.

*   *   *

She awakened, her bright eyes exposed to this new environment. Blood trickled down her fragile face. She shuffled within the engulfing pile of fresh hay – sitting up slowly as pieces of the sweet straw fell from her dark matted hair. Rae had no recall of what happened and how she ended up in this darkened forest. Silence covered the air like a blanket.

"Where ...am I? ... Mum? ... Dad?" she muttered, scanning her surroundings.

She sniffled, unsure and scared of this place that seemed darker than Hell.

The silence was broken. The sudden distant sound of thundering hooves of horses grew rapidly louder. Her gentle breathing increased into panting. *What was this threatening sound?* Hunters. Hunters in search of young Rae. She caught a glimpse of their sharp weapons and threatening expressions before spreading her muffled wings and fleeing from the storm.

The thundering hooves grew closer and closer as Rae's wings grew weaker and weaker She meandered through the towering trees and the sharpened spears that were trying to pierce her. The roaring voices were beneath her. Rae could not escape any longer. She knew that eventually, her wings would give in. And they did. The swift gliding turned to falling as she collapsed in a pile of damp leaves. The hooves came to a stop – their chains rattling at the sudden halt. The hunters dismounted their steeds. Rae could hear the threatening sound of spears being drawn. Her heart sank. She briskly shuffled in the leaf pile in an attempt to escape. But it was too late. The hunters surrounded her – positioning their spears at the winged creature shaking in front of them. Rae's eyes widened and she panted heavily. The young angel pushed herself against the tree, blocking her escape as she trembled with fear.

"W-What do you want from me?" Rae cried out.

"Silence, you monster," one of the hunters bellowed.

"M-monster…?" she muttered.

"I said SILENCE!"

The hunter hurled their spear – piercing it through Rae's wing. She let out a shriek of pain – the blood gushed out of the wound. The hunter lifted Rae by the neck and took out a freshly sharpened dagger. She whimpered.

"SILENCE!" he yelled, as he sliced her bare skin.

She cried out again. Another hunter began chaining Rae's limbs together. Rae did not dare to make another sound. The pain was already a heavy burden. They mounted her to the tree – hanging her by the frail bones of her wings. The five hunters all gathered around her. Every one wielded a dagger. Slash! Slash! They each drew blood from cuts on her chained limbs. Tears streamed down the young angel's face. She was slowly losing the will to fight back. Would she be saved, or would she continue to suffer within this torture?

Her breathing grew slower, and the daggers still nipped her flesh. Rae's limbs were coated with layers of her dripping blood, staining her worn-down clothes. She could feel the daggers digging closer to her bones. It was too painful for her to fight for her life. At this point, Rae was giving into her death. Maybe sending her from heaven was pointless. The eternal slumber was coming within reach. The young angel had her eyes shut while the hunters cut away at her bloody flesh.

But what was that faint sound she heard? It almost sounded like the twinkle of a fairy although it was surely impossible for mythical creatures to be on Earth. It was indeed a twinkle, growing louder by the second. Rae used the last of her strength to look along the stretched pathway of forest.

There, looming silently behind the hunters, was a hooded being. They wielded what seemed to be a long branch with a glow on top. A staff? Rae's vision was too blurred to know what this mysterious being was. Were they the one to save the angel from her torture, or was this a second enemy that also planned to execute her? Their clothing was dark and matted although it wasn't as damaged as Rae's. The young angel could slightly make out a face – it was wrinkled and capped with a mass of grey hair. It seemed to be an elderly woman. She lifted her twisted staff and with a single thud to the forest floor, the hunters slowly began to fade into nothing.

It was a miracle.

Rae couldn't process what had happened in that split second, but she knew that she was safe once again. The elderly woman carefully removed the chains from her limbs and took her in their arms.

"It's okay, young one. I'm here to protect you from all the beasts in this vile world."

Rae was brought to a shack located in the centre of the dark forest. A small gap in the trees shone upon the place where the elderly woman lived. This area of the forest was more aesthetically pleasing than its surroundings. Animals thrived and freshly bloomed flowers stood proudly. It was a shock to Rae as a young white-haired girl approached her swiftly. Her eyes were a vibrant purple that shone purely.

"Is this the angel you were talking about, Grandma?" the girl yelled in excitement.

"Calm down dear, poor thing almost died out there."

"Sorry Grandma…"

Rae was gently rested onto a professionally made bed, where the girl loomed over her whilst holding her hand out.

"I'm Sylv."

Rae weakly rested her hand in Sylv's.

"Rae."

"Ooh, that's a pretty name!"

The young angel was already feeling warmth in this place. This place, with Sylv and Grandma, would be where she would be welcomed the most.

IDENTITY UNKNOWN
BY LAURA DEViNE

I woke up on the floor. My head was throbbing. I can't remember
how I got here. *Think, Mae, think.* I stood up, my cheeks burning
as I inhaled the air around me, taking in the surroundings. As I
breathed out, it seemed to echo around the walls. Blood pounded
against my head even harder. I sensed something familiar around.
There were iron-barred windows with the glass panes missing. A
shattering wind seared through me. I stumbled backwards, almost
sitting on the iron bed. I only just noticed it now. It was iron and
rusty. My fingers brushed against it causing a burning sensation
across my skin. I felt a shiver down my spine. In confusion, I
stumbled around trying to escape. There was no door, but I felt
like I was being pulled back, drawn to the bed. I couldn't sit on
that bed; I just knew I couldn't. It seemed to be getting closer. I
was running, faster and faster away from this. I screamed from

the bottom of my lungs. Darkness swirled around me like a foggy pillow, suffocating me. I tried to push it away with a piercing wail. In one last attempt to push away the spirit taunting me, I loudly and calmly said, "Stop."

Everything seemed to slow down, I thought it was all over, but I looked around and before I knew it I was sitting on the bed. I gasped. I tried to get up, but I was being pushed back down.

*　*　*

"Identity unknown."

My head was throbbing.

"17:33, an unrecognised girl was found."

A deathly scream shot through my head.

"Two stab wounds in the chest."

A metallic taste engulfed my throat.

"Her identity unrecorded."

Blood trickled out of my nose.

"Repeat: Her identity unrecorded."

I screamed, but it disappeared when it reached my lips. I was unsure whether I was alive or dead.

The trees whispered, saying my name over and over, chanting, getting louder and louder, faster and faster, shouting, screaming, mocking me. I lifted my hand to my face. My skin was peeling, melting away. My worst nightmare. An electric shock shot through me. My eyes were burning, sweat dripping down the nape of my neck. I looked at my hand. It was shaking. I suddenly became aware of how heavily I was breathing. I was laying on an iron bed. I stood up, every bone in my body protesting. I had blood on my shirt and my skin was bruised and burnt.

I tried to scream. A silent scream. I couldn't remember anything. I couldn't even remember how to be scared. Words were turning in my head, letters swirling, not in the right place.

d I e t y i n t … unknown. My first memory flooded back to me, drowning me with realisation.

"Identity unknown."

The unknown murder. I couldn't remember how many minutes it had been since then. Could be hours, weeks, even years, and I wouldn't know. Suddenly I felt so tired, exhausted, all the energy draining out of me. I collapsed on the floor, unconscious.

When I woke up again, all the letters in my head had joined up. I could remember again! Sentences, words, letters, mounting up. Still on the iron bed, I rolled over and tried to stand up.

Except.

My entire body was bound to the floor in iron chains.

I gasped out loud.

"Who are you?" I whispered.

The uncanny voices echoed back at me. Somewhere, a single voice replied to me, multiplying, bouncing off the walls, mocking me, engulfing me, suffocating me.

"You know why you're here. And you will lose your stupid bet."

The bet. With Amelie.

I remember my friend's voice, laughing, pure joy, her face dancing round the room.

"I bet you won't find out who did it."

I was inhaling my memories, collecting in my head. My heart was racing. *I can fix this,* I thought. *But first, how did I get here?* The party. The guilt flooded me. Suddenly my thoughts were dissolving, the words melting. I desperately tried to keep them together.

I was at Josh's party.

Amelie's boyfriend's party.

He bought me a drink.

It tasted strange but I drank it anyway.

Then it hit me.

My best friend's boyfriend spiked my drink.

I gasped.

Anger surged through me flooding my veins. I needed to think. Create a plan. Get revenge.

Two weeks prior, an unknown person had gone missing. Her body was found dead in the woods. I don't think that the identity was unknown. I think it was censored.

"Mae."

I gasped, the voice cutting through my thoughts. A voice I recognised.

"Josh," I whispered, barely audible in reply.

Silence.

Footsteps.

I looked around trying to locate the voice and the footsteps. They were uneven footsteps, like a limp. Another memory uncovered itself in my head. Amelie mentioned Josh was having a fight with someone, but I blacked out before it happened.

I thought I had imagined it at first, but the cold metal chains still bound me to the bed. I pulled the chains behind my back, twisting them. Every chain loop had a gap where it joined itself. If I untwisted it enough I could break the chains and escape.

Suddenly, a dark fleeting thought crossed through my head. *What if this was how he killed his last victim?*

It took me a minute to realise but ... *was Josh the killer?* Mae, stop it. Concentrate. I twisted the chains even harder. The more they resisted, the more enraged I got. My blood boiled through my veins, sweat trickled across my brow. Time seemed to slow down and speed up at the same time.

A scream escaped my throat – not a silent one, a proper one. I forced my hands open, and the chains clattered to the ground. *Not the best idea to only have chains bound at one place Josh,* I thought. I had to get out of here before Josh could get me. I raced out, the icy gusts of wind searing through my hair. I saw the entrance doors looming in the distance. I could hear my feet crashing against the ground, but I just had to get out.

Then I came to a stop.

Josh. A barricade between me and the outside, freedom.

Normally I would just shove him over but ... this was the person who spiked my drink ...

The anger I felt drowned the fear.

But then he started walking. He limped, waddled over to me. His arm was in a cast. Before I could even think about it, a laugh escaped my lips, getting louder until I didn't know why I was laughing.

"Why are you laughing?"

His icy tone cut off my laugh.

"Aww poor you, you lost your fight," surprising myself with the tone I used.

He looked annoyed and sighed. I went to walk past him, but he simply put his hand out and said, "Wait."

I stopped in my tracks.

"You're telling me to wait__"

He cut me off.

"Stop. If you tell the police I killed that girl, Amelie's life is ruined."

My pulse quickened.

"What do you mean?"

"She supplied me with the drugs I used to spike your drink."

My world slowed to a stop.

My best friend.

My muscles froze up, like they do when you die. I had to choose. Me or Amelie. Like he had read my thoughts, he replied to them.

"The choice is all yours."

He turned to walk away, his stupid limp mocking his steps.

"Wait!" I said. "Did Amelie know you were going to give them to me?"

"I__" Josh replied.

The guilt on his stupid face was enough to answer my question. Rage filled me again. Betrayal. I shoved past him, not waiting when he told me to this time. I ran and ran and raced till I got home. I can't even remember how I knew the way. All I remember is Josh falling to the floor, calling out in agony.

No one was home but I probably wouldn't have noticed if they were.

"999, what's your emergency?"

I guess Amelie was going to lose the bet this time.

ESS
OF E

This project started with a question: *What does Eerie mean to you?*

NCE
ERIE

Here are some initial responses…

Tunnels by Katie

The darkness. Something about it just makes me want to turn and run but somehow I can't. The darkness of the tunnel lured me inside, wanting me to enter, wanting me to feel insecure. I can't run. I'm almost frozen, my mobility snatched from me I need to get away from the tunnel but instead of running I find myself stumbling forward, entering the deathly silence. Run, I'm telling myself. Run away. I'm scared. The walls of the tunnel seemed to be creeping closer and closer. I'm trapped. There's no escape. There's daylight blinking at me towards the end of the tunnel. I go to run forward, but I run into something solid, something blocking my route to freedom. I'm not going to escape.

North Mills Trading Estate at Night by Toby

Even the most piercing eyes could not scathe the darkness which surrounds me. When there is silence, the world around you feels still bustling and busy. Like standing on a knife edge, one wrong move could be the last. Torches seem to add eeriness when in use because it shows how limited your vision is compared to the world which surrounds you. Like lightning, people think it strikes the earth, but it is trying to escape from the ground. However, it is stopped by the shield of atmosphere that cloaks the earth. We fixate on the silence. We forget to concentrate on the world around us so when the sound of footsteps, or the glass bottle being knocked over which had just been put down before, these things intimidate us like a hungry wolf sneaking up on its prey through the woods.

My Farm by Katie

I can stand at the top of the hill, not being able to see what is around me, carefully treading, so that the vast darkness can't send me venturing off in the opposite direction. The holes are everywhere, past footsteps of cows that roam around in the darkness. The darkness is almost like a demon, it waits to snatch its prey off guard.

The Bathroom by Laura

When I step into the bathroom, and icy cold gust hits me. The hinges on the door creak, breaking the silence. It takes me by surprise, and I gasp. I hear it echoing but it might just be in my head. I step inside the room; I hear the faint buzzing of the heating. I look up from my phone to see my reflection in the mirror. I get a shiver down my spine. Ugh, I'm being so stupid, I think. I pull the rope to turn on the light. Nothing happens. My heart starts thumping in my chest. I turn around to leave but just then the light flickers into action. The door suddenly bangs itself shut. Beads of sweat start trickling down the back of my neck. In my peripheral vision I can see the rope I pulled, swinging. I can smell the dust and I feel like cobwebs are wrapping around me, suffocating. I sprint out of the room, gasping.

The Autopsy by Laura and Summer

They looked unique
unknown in Greece

possible suicide
but looks like murder

washed up on the beach
most likely drowned by the sea

but contradicting injuries
broken shoulder, dented head

nail scratches around neck
a single rip but
otherwise, perfect

smudged lipstick and ripped out hair
different coloured eyes, different personalities

the watch states the time of death
precisely 12 o'clock
a printed note in his fingers

"murder or suicide?" asked P.C. Parsons

"suicide,' I replied. "it has to be"

Graveyard by Talia

I wandered around the graveyard shivering, asking myself why I'd been abandoned. It was the middle of November and the middle of the night. I anxiously looked around but saw nothing but darkness. I despised this. I crept up the concrete path in the direction I thought the church might be. I held my hands out like a zombie and soon enough, found myself grasping the iron gates that denied anyone from getting to the church door. I was trapped like a tiger. I heard a twig crack and a crunch of leaves. Then I heard what seemed to be a giggle of some boys, probably a couple of years older than me. They were stumbling around kicking leaves, until one grabbed my shoulder and stabbed something into my neck. I cried out, quickly raising my hand to the pain. The boy still gripped the blade, his hand twitching slightly. Then he spoke, a hint of spite in his tone.

"Don't you know this is our land? That people like you end up deader than the people in this graveyard. Don't you know?"

His hand was constantly jerking as he spoke so violently. I started to feel lightheaded. I felt the slick, warm blood slide down my arm and back. The boy sharply slid the blade out of my neck, and I collapsed, grasping the wound as tightly as I could. My breathing was hoarse as I lay there unable to think properly. My father had abandoned me in a graveyard, and I got stabbed. I couldn't think of anything worse. My eyes felt heavy, and my mind went blank. I passed out.

Foggy Beaches by Summer

All I can hear all I can hear is the crash of the wave and the
howl of the wind telling me to 'Go, run, run fast!' There isn't
a person in sight, but there must be because I can hear their
breath cutting through the wind and the crunch of their
footsteps on the rocky sand. I look over my shoulder: no one.
It must be me imagining again but it's getting louder. What is
happening? Am I going insane? I check over my shoulder: no
one. Then I hear it. A bloodcurdling scream. Before I realise
what I am doing, I'm sprinting towards it, but nothing is
coming. No one is here. I spin on the spot and then everything
goes black.

Threats* by Samuel

Footsteps

Quiet bang going on constantly,

Getting closer to you

Ghostly

Dead figures lurking around,

Moving very silently

Thunder

Loud bangs covering the sky,

And a sudden flash from nowhere

Woods by Samuel

Whenever I see or go in some woods, I always get that eerie sort of feel whenever it's misty, as the mist always wraps around the trees and glides through the undergrowth, and you can't really see where you are. It always makes you feel you are the only person there or nearby, and everything else is really still or quiet. All you can hear is your feet crunching on the leaves. Whenever I go deeper into the woods the mist always seems to get thicker and thicker. I walk forward, deeper into the thick foggy mist and I step on a dead branch from a tree lying there. SNAP! Then it echoes around the whole entire woods, and it feels like everything is staring at you as you struggle through the piled up dead leaves and branches to go further down. Will this journey ever end? I asked myself, not knowing if it will or not. It all seems to be a bit far-fetched. All I can see is just thick white clouds and the dark outline of trees in the distance, and the very faint sound of water in the distance from a nearby stream, rushing past the stones and falling down a little waterfall and floating downstream.

The Moors by Ella

I approach a mass of stones and trees, the rot smell sinking into the slimy brown goop, trees surrounding me, the illusion, the eyes…I feel as if I am an actor in a TV show being watched: every move, every step, every breath faster than the previous. I have to get out. It seems like an endless maze, ever expanding; it taunts me, a noise, a step, and then black. Nothing.

IKEA by Evie

I stroll through each stretching aisle, the tall ceiling looming above me. I begin to zone out the longer I hear the repetitive music. The exit must be nearby, it must be. I've been waiting for what feels like days now. I take turn after turn, but I always end up where I began – somewhere. Where is somewhere? I don't know myself. Somewhere looks the same as everywhere. Every corner is the same. Every aisle is the same. I must be losing my mind here but yet again, I don't know. My legs eventually begin to weaken. My eyes closed shut as I collapsed to the hard floor. My mind is now blacked out. I see nothing. But I hear something. It sounds like the distant sound of whispers engulfing me. Is this all a nightmare? I still don't know.

Libraries by Riley

Libraries have a smell of dust and old sightings which gives the vision of an antique house that has peculiar noises, which eventually become worrying or infuriating due to the noises being unknown. Libraries are also eerie because it's always silent, which you have to be. This feeling gives the indication that something bad will happen if you aren't quiet. The librarians can also be intimidating because of the fact that they don't speak and rarely move; it doesn't seem like they are a real person, more in comparison to a controlled animatronic, who is forced to sit and live its life there. If the librarian does ever go out of sight, the feeling intensifies as you are most likely on your own.

Poundbury by Mani

I have never been comfortable in places that felt as if they had
been scrubbed clean, places that had no soul, no life. I walked
among the buildings. Their mere presence put me on edge.
The coldness that emanated from them was overpowering. I
am sure this bleak style of house attracted people, but there
never seemed to be any signs of life. No encouraging warmth,
no movement except for shadows that appeared if you stared
for too long. The sea of grey and beige stretched as far as the
eye could see. It felt as though the houses had no intention of
letting people inhabit them. The rough texture of the bricks was
off-putting and almost aggressive. I yearned for colour, for the
smell of life, the feeling of community. But this place would not
offer it. The houses refused.

Museum by Mani

The museum was empty. She sat, letting the silence wash over
her, the artificial lighting emphasised the coldness of the room.
The book she had been reading lay on the floor. Abandoned.
She didn't mind being alone; she enjoyed her own company
but today something felt different. Out of place. Her manager
would have said it was because of the mercury retrograde. She
got up and stretched. She longed for movement. She began to
wander around. Her footsteps echoed throughout the room.
Her breath bounced off the walls returning to her twice as loud.
The painting at the back of the room beckoned to her.
Its whispers travelled through the air. Her pace quickened.
Her manner changed – she now had a purpose.

Walking your Dog at Night by Jade

I'm walking my dog at night through the park. It's dark and misty, cold, a slight dim from the streetlamps. There are people walking around or sat on a bench under the trees. Just sitting there. People shouldn't be out at night in the cold and dark. Also, when people are walking their dog at night, they watch me as I go past or when a dog bark echoes in the distance. When I hear shouting when I'm out at night, my dog stops and stares in one direction and watches, but I can't see anything there. When a light flickers in the dark like a street lamp, or when a line of lights except one is always flickering but the others aren't. I also find pictures creepy and eerie when it feels like they're staring into your soul.

Any Shady Corner by Danny

I saw the shady dark corner. There were some shady figures in the shady, gloomy, and dark corner. One of the shady figures was holding a bag and the other was holding piles of cash. The bag was small, but the cash was big. It was a lot of money, but what were they trying to buy? What was in the bag? The shady figures started moving but they looked like someone had sucked the sleep out of them. Their eyes were bloodshot red, and they were moving weirdly like they forgot how to walk straight.

The Hotel by Chandler

The long corridor with abstract patterns on the wall that acts like a maze. The flickering lights by every door. The silence of the corridor never seems to end. The not knowing what surprises wait for you behind the door. What's behind the door? Scared that the strip light may not work. Looking through the window just to see a shady corner within an abandoned building. You never really can tell what a hotel will be like.

Abandoned Places by Emily

I walk through the dusty hallway. It goes on forever – almost like it will never end. I feel trapped and scared and like I can't ever escape this horrific nightmare. I hear noises coming from deep down inside of the basement. Although this house is thought to have been abandoned, I somehow don't believe it. The floorboards creak as I venture nearer to the basement door. I run my finger along the dust-ridden bannister of the staircase. The house must be old. The air tastes bitter and thick and my mouth is dry. The walls are colourless, and the paintings are of faces. Familiar, pale faces. I know I have been here before... but when? All of this feels too unreal and strange. I feel watched! Could this house be haunted? Shrill screams echo in my ear. Is it all in my head...? I turned to look outside. I peered through the murky glass. Waves crashing and cracking along the shore like a whip. The melancholy sky hangs low, looming over the dark sea. The house sways. The strong winds howl. I panic as I hear the noise again.

Any London Train Station by Coe

The never-ending suspense of not knowing what's going to happen. Be it day or night, the feeling is still the same. Watching your back, suspenseful of what's to come. The stench of marijuana in the air as you hear the tin cans and crisp packets beneath your feet. And lighting is invaded by a sharp beam of light and a heavy chattering. A train rushes past. The groans of beggars on the street combined with the laughs of teenagers. You glance at the billboard to check your schedule. The train arrives and you step on it, only to experience the same thing tomorrow.

Underground Car Parks by Zoe

As my old and peculiar car pulled into the stacked four-storey car park situated beneath the streets of the smoky city above, chugging along, the vehicle began to come to a slow halt. A tight area marked out by faint, chalky lines painted onto the concrete, that had worn away over the many years that the structure had been standing. I turned off the engine and the car gave a small groan. As if it was anxious to be there. I hesitantly pulled the door to my right open and took a step out onto the rough concrete. The vast area at the bottom floor of the car park was dimly lit by the overhead lights, of which their cover had accumulated dust and debris. Some were off, and many were mildly flickering. It was as if I could sense the three storeys above me, like they were closing in on me. My eyes quickly caught the first but singular elevator. I began to walk. My tapping steps getting faster and faster by the second. Until the elevator doors slid open. The ping sounded and the noise bounced throughout the car park, and a tall figure stood below the red light inside the elevator.

Morrisons by Freya

This place is a nightmare! Everywhere you turn more people and noise. You can't escape. You can feel the tension thick in the air mixed with the smell of freshly baked bread creating an unpleasant aroma, which makes you want to recoil in disgust. But you can't. You have to keep going, you've got to escape. You can hear the footsteps, faint, getting louder and closer. You can see the door. You can feel the fresh air. You are nearly free. But you feel the darkness coil around your ankles pulling you back. You struggle, but your attempts at freeing yourself are useless. You are one of them now.

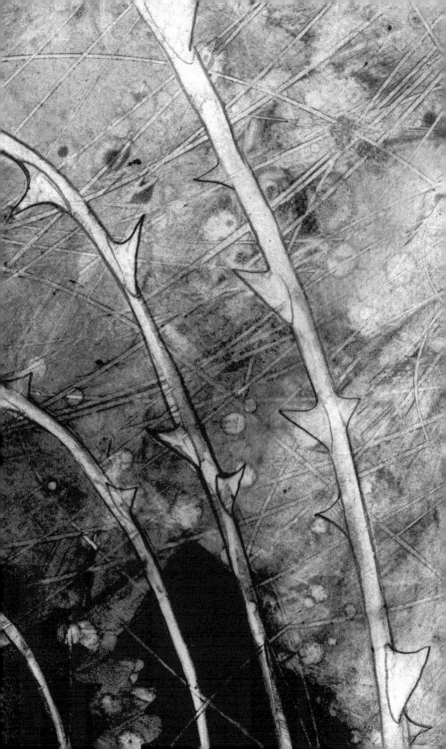

THE
BANK
OF
DREAMS

NIGHT
MARES

SPIRALLING
A SLOW DESCENT INTO MADNESS

This anthology is the culmination of six weekly sessions with a group of Year 9 pupils from Sir John Colfox School in Bridport. We started by asking a simple question:

What do you find eerie?

From this, we gathered that eerie means very different things to different people, from hotel corridors and underground tube stations to deserted libraries and the maze that is IKEA. Some of those initial thoughts are in this book, and they started a wonderful six-week writing conversation with these teenagers.

Our purpose was to provide the young writers with the toolkit to write freely, with the outcome of a published book based around that eerie theme. The writing process is messy and non-linear, and each student was given a journal to explore that process, unhindered by thoughts of marking, grading, or assessment. The pupils were uniquely placed to explore their ideas with volunteer Writing Mentors assigned to small groups; without the support of Amberley Carter, Nick Goldsmith, Eleanor James, and Raja Jarrah, the anthology would not be what it is.

We developed writing craft by looking at poetry by Simon Armitage and explored how character might be 'shown' by the things they carry with them. We enjoyed word play by creating eerie Kenning poems – an Anglo-Saxon language form that really makes the reader think. And we spent several weeks building the short stories that are published here, from initial inspiration, to planning the story arc, peer feedback, expert feedback, and the all-important editing process. It takes real stamina to write a short story and stay with it to cut, polish, and fine tune, and these young writers demonstrated that stamina in abundance.

The Bank of Dreams & Nightmares' ethos is to offer child-led creative writing workshops, to listen to young people, and learn from them. By offering small group mentoring as we did here, children are given time and space; what they have to say and write is nothing short of remarkable.

It's a credit to Sir John Colfox School to recognise the power and impact this kind of enrichment can have; special mention goes to Liz Launder for co-ordinating the entire project with us, with thanks to headteacher Adam Shelley for having us. And big thanks to Kate Shelley in the library, who offered such a warm welcome each week, as well as tea and coffee!

The final title you see on the cover of this anthology is the result of a collaborative decision by the students themselves, and perfectly encapsulates the imagination, creativity, and turmoil that resides within its pages. We are immensely proud of the Colfox writers; Spiralling: A Descent into Madness is testament to their engagement and the creative spark that is unique to young minds.

Jan Lane
Creative Learning Manager
The Bank of Dreams & Nightmares

ABOUT THE BANK OF DREAMS & NIGHTMARES

OUR MISSION STATEMENT

Everyone's full of stories. Don't believe me? Well then off to bed
and see for yourself. For when you sleep the stories in your head
wake up. Your dreams and nightmares come alive and start to play
in a world of infinite possibility and never-ending imagination.
And then you wake up. And reality brings them crashing to an
end, cruelly concluding all that could have been. Well we're here
to put an end to that, or at least a beginning. 1000s and 1000s
of beginnings. Hear ye hear ye! We at the Bank of Dreams &
Nightmares want your stories. Bring them in, in all their absurd,
weird and wonderful starts, middles or ends. And we'll keep your
story alive, keep it going, bringing it out of your head and into the
cold but illuminating light of day. And we won't stop there. Oh
no. Every story deposited in the Bank of Dreams & Nightmares
gets interest. Like any good bank we'll help your investment grow
and grow. We'll give it eyes and ears to see and hear it, words to
appreciate it, and applause to motivate it on. So believe in what's
in your head, believe in what you can create, believe in your dreams
and nightmares.

OUR AIM

get more kids writing and show them just
how far their words can take them.

BY

making them realise their weird, wonderful,
absurd, ridiculous ideas are all story-worthy

PROMISING

that if they deposit them in our bank we'll bring
them to life and help them accrue interest
(i.e. eyes and ears to see and hear them)

THE INSPIRATION

Valencia 826 in San Francisco

WHAT WE DO

We are a registered charity in West Dorset and we offer FREE
creative writing workshops to children aged 7-18 in the West
Dorset area of the UK. We want to show children just how far
their words and stories can take them, so we work with industry
professionals to create inspirational workshops that all have a
real world outcome. How about writing a campaign for a cause
you feel strongly about and then seeing it made by professionals
so you can present it to local government or businesses? What if
you wrote some song lyrics, and then are able to see a real musical
artist take your words and make it into a real recording you can

share with the world? Or how about you become the lead defence lawyer for a special mock trial in a real court house where your persuasive arguments determine whether someone is guilty or not guilty? The possibilities are endless and at The Bank of Dreams & Nightmares; we want to have fun showing children that it all starts with an idea, a story, some words and where that can take you is the exciting part.

Our focus is on those children who are most under resourced, who normally do not have access to these types of things but deserve them just as much as anyone else.

We will be housed in a real bank in Bridport, but instead of money, we deal in the currency of stories, and at the back of the store, if you know where to look, is a secret door that leads to the writing centre where the real magic happens.

We work with both primary and secondary schools during term time providing one-off story writing workshops with the end result being published authors or broadcast podcasts! We also work in collaboration with secondary schools to develop longer term long projects where the outcome is a published anthology of the young writers' stories.

We offer after school clubs for children to develop their writing and get involved in longer workshop projects that currently range from creating their own quarterly newspaper to a sketch comedy workshop, with the final sketches being made by professional actors.

The Bank of Dreams & Nightmares is committed to practically addressing educational inequalities and the opportunity gap faced by young people from less advantaged backgrounds. We work in communities with high levels of socio-economic inequality, where we are providing a critical link between local schools, arts organisations, higher education institutions, and the commercial sector.

Our aim is to help children and young people to discover and harness the power of their own imaginations and creative writing skills. The Bank of Dreams & Nightmares strives to improve children's behaviour, engagement, essential life skills and wellbeing - the root causes of exclusion.

At its core The Bank of Dreams & Nightmares is also about something much broader and more inclusive: it is about using the creative practice of writing and storytelling to strengthen local children and teenagers from all backgrounds, to be resilient, creative, and successful shapers of their own lives.

IMPACT

Through our programmes, young writers will have felt listened to and have had their opinions valued and acted upon. We can demonstrate the impact creative writing has on young people. We provoke and empower them to think creatively and help them to unlock their imaginations. Then we publish their writing, providing purpose and value. The impact will demonstrate significant shifts in motivation, attitude, and behaviours - which in turn affects health, ambition, and resilience.

OUR WORKSHOPS

Primary School
Storymaking workshop

In this two and a half hour workshop we work with a class collectively to create a story, whilst one of our volunteer illustrators brings the story to life as it happens. The first half of the session has the class of young writers voting and creating as a group, as one of our volunteers scribes the story for them. Once they get to the cliffhanger moment each writer then creates their own ending to the story, with the help of our story mentors. After the session we take the words and pictures and make them into a beautiful bound book with each participant getting their own author biog at the back and space to finish their individual ending. It is always a fun and lively session and the results have been wonderful.

Secondary School
Podcasting workshop

In this one-off workshop we work with a class of young writers to develop a personal essay about identity. The workshop normally lasts around four hours as we explore different aspects of the self and what it means to our writers. It is always a lively and interactive session and the final outcome is to record each essay as a podcast, which is broadcast via our soundcloud page.

Secondary School
Six Week Story Anthology

In this longer programme we work with one group of students to develop an anthology based on a chosen theme. We work closely with the school to decide on a theme which complements the curriculum for the chosen year group. At the end of the six weeks we make the final anthology into a published book, one of which you are reading now. All the proceeds from the sales of the book go directly back into the charity.

The Vault Newspaper

This is our after school workshop that takes place every Thursday during term time after school. Here we work with a group of young writers between 10 and 15 years of age to create a quarterly subscription-based newspaper. In the issue we look back at the news from the last three months and the writers share their perspectives on the news stories that they have selected.

We have many more workshops being developed, and will hopefully be able to share them with you all very soon.

PEOPLE

Founder
Nick Goldsmith

Creative learning manager
Janis Lane

Volunteer Coordinator
Alex Green

Board of Directors
Mick Smith
Simon Deverell
Joel Collins
Niki McCretton
Simon Hawkins

OUR VOLUNTEERS

There is absolutely no way any of this would be possible without our incredible volunteers. These incredible people work in all realms from story mentoring to illustrating and beyond. They range in age, background and expertise but all have a shared passion for our work with young people. We salute you!

IT'S ALWAYS A GOOD TIME TO GIVE

WE NEED YOUR HELP

We are always seeking new volunteers to help out either as story mentors, illustrators, or simply as experts in their fields. It is very simple to join as a volunteer, and we try and make it a lot of fun in the process. You do not need to be a writer or have an educational background, you just need to be able to listen and encourage our young writers to express themselves.

Please fill out our online application to let us know how you may be able to help, and to come along to one of our training sessions. Tea and cake provided!

More information at thebankofdreamsandnightmares.org/volunteering

OTHER WAYS TO GIVE

Whether it's loose change or heaps of cash, a donation of any size will help The Bank of Dreams & Nightmares continue to offer a variety of FREE writing workshops to children in the West Dorset area. Please make a donation at:
thebankofdreamsandnightmares.org/donate

Or email us at nick@thebankofdreamsandnightmares.org
to discuss how you may be able to help.

All proceeds from the sale of
this book go toward funding
free student programming
at The Bank of Dreams &
Nightmares.

Spiralling: A slow descent into
madness has been made possible
with the generous help of

**Other books available from the vaults at
The Bank of Dreams & Nightmares:**

"I HAVE A DREAM"
by young writers at Beaminster school

I was driving through Beaminster recently and it was a normal busy weekday morning, people popping into shops, chatting on the street, going about their business. Little did I know that just up the road The Bank of Dreams and Nightmares was roaring, exploding, clattering into action in Beaminster School, firing up this extraordinary collection of stories. Pouring out of the school into the bright Dorset morning were these tales of betrayal, yearning, adventure, jeopardy, cold-blooded murder and chilling suspense. Extract from foreword by Max Porter

Books are available at Little Toller Books in Beaminster and The Book Shop in Bridport plus online via our website: **www.thebankofdreamsandnightmares.org**

All proceeds go directly into funding more workshops run by the charity.

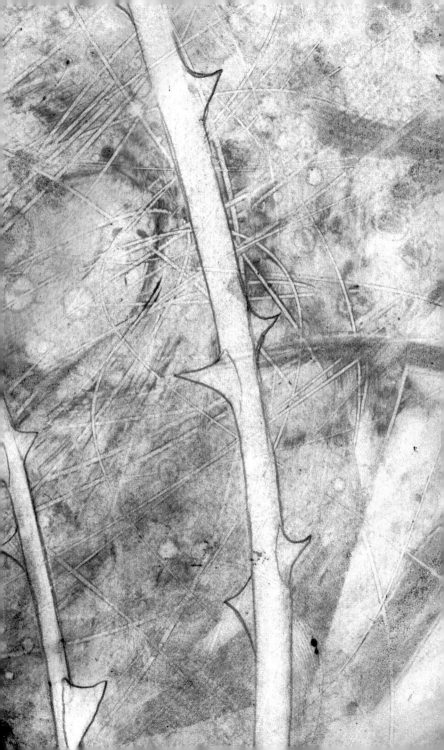

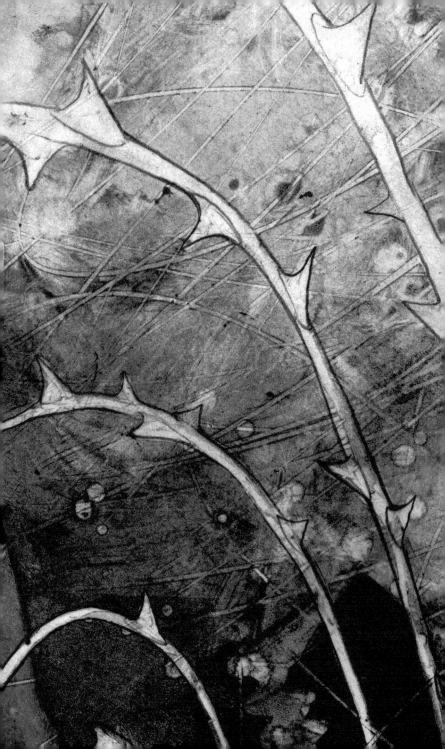